THE CONCIERGE

MIRANDA RIJKS

INKUBATOR
BOOKS

Published by Inkubator Books
www.inkubatorbooks.com

Copyright © 2022 by Miranda Rijks

ISBN (eBook): 978-1-83756-048-6
ISBN (Paperback): 978-1-83756-049-3
ISBN (Hardback): 978-1-83756-050-9

Miranda Rijks has asserted her right to be identified as the
author of this work.

CONTENTS

1

SIMONE

My phone pings with an incoming text.

Sorry, S, but I won't be able to make it tonight. I can't get off in time. Forgive me?? Axxx

I groan. I've made a roast chicken stuffed with dried apricots, dates and nuts, Ally's favourite meal, and now I'm going to have to eat it all alone and have chicken every day for the next week. It's nearly 8 pm, and this was meant to be our special evening, a long overdue catch-up.

'Oh, Ally,' I murmur as I switch off the oven. 'I hope this is all worth it.' It hasn't passed me by that I'm turning into a demented spinster, living alone and talking to myself. Having discovered my last boyfriend had been cheating on me for quite possibly the entire length of our two-year relationship, I'm done with dating. I glance at Ally's text message again. My sister has changed dramatically in the past three months, and I'm worried about her. She knows I'm a stickler for timekeeping, and she knows that nothing triggers me more than someone bailing out at the last minute for no good reason. Yet this has been her pattern for weeks now. Perhaps this is par for the course when you're on the cusp of fame. I just hope she's not going to be pushed into forgoing her core values. Ally and I may be very different, but we share the same principles; at least I've always thought we did.

The one thing we differ on is patience. I'm one of those people who gets fidgety in a queue, who feels a welling up of raw impatience when someone is late. It's ironic, really, because I'm British through and through, and as a nation we're meant to be so good at queuing. Being an actress, Ally is the epitome of patience and perseverance, which is probably why she's being catapulted to fame with this new role she's in while I'm slogging away as a self-employed bookkeeper.

She's the pretty English rose with thick wavy blonde hair, blue eyes and rosebud lips. I have Dad's features: mousy hair, which I dye a shade of auburn, cut short and choppy to make my dark eyes look bigger. No one's actually been brave enough to ask me outright whether I'm jealous of my sister, with her fine looks and talent, along with her doting husband and doll-like daughter, but the honest answer is no. I love Ally. We're more than sisters: although it sounds trite to say so, we're best friends. There's no one in the world whom I am more proud of, whom I adore so unreservedly than my younger sister. And although I'm annoyed with her for pulling out of supper at the last minute, I know it's through no fault of her own. Ally hasn't got a malicious bone in her body.

I send her a message back.

Come over any time before midnight and don't let them work you too hard! Xx

I grab my navy oven gloves and take the chicken out. It

smells delicious, and I cut myself a large slice. Cooking is my hobby, not that I have the chance to share my culinary creations with many people these days. Most of my friends are married with young children, and the relaxed dinner parties of old that drifted into the early hours are long passed. My focus these days is on my business, if you can call it that. I earn reasonable money from my bunch of loyal accountancy clients. It's not exciting, but it keeps me going.

I turn the television on, but it doesn't hold my attention. I'm worried about Ally. She's been trying for years to get a leading actor role, and neither Rob, her husband, nor I had the heart to dash her dreams. She's attended hundreds, if not thousands of auditions and has played bit parts here and there, but nothing that equated to the talent that her drama tutors identified back when she was a student. If I'm being honest, I thought at thirty-two it was never going to happen for her, so when she was cast by Delucci Productions as one of their leading roles in a new film, no one was more delighted than me. It's her big break. If this film is a box office hit, then Ally will be firmly on the ladder. But it's come at a cost, and the last few months have been horrendous. Ally has been working eighteen-hour days. She's barely seen Rob or Carly, and she's racked with guilt that she only sees her little girl when she is fast asleep. I last saw Ally three weeks ago, and I was shocked at how much weight she'd lost, how mauve the rings were under her eyes. I suppose it's the stress and those long hours. I shared my concerns with Rob, but what can we do? This role is the possible culmination of a lifelong dream. Rob has always been very supportive of how close Ally and I are and has been accommodating of our weekly Monday night suppers. That's a joke – they haven't been weekly for months.

At least three weeks ago, Ally was on time.

'Bloody hell, All, are you alright?' I'd asked as I stared at her skinny arms and sunken cheeks.

'Yeah, I'm fine.' She leaned in for a kiss.

'You're skin and bones.'

'Ha. No time for food on set.'

'But you've got to eat. Surely they want healthy-looking actors.'

'It's the hours,' she said, wriggling her fingers at me and striding towards the oven. 'Something smells scrumptious.'

She spent the evening diverting conversation away from herself towards me, or talking about Carly, a topic we were both comfortable with. All I gleaned was that she was working crazy hours and was patently exhausted. Ally's never been one for gossip, but I really was hoping for a bit more insight into the cast and crew, and particularly Goldie and Braun Delucci, the power couple behind the production. But no. Ally was tight-lipped.

At 10 pm, I send my sister another message and wait for the little ticks to change colour, but nothing happens. After ten minutes I accept that poor Ally is still filming. I feel sorry for Rob. He's essentially a single parent at the moment, and I wonder how sustainable that is. I hope that Ally has thought about it, that this is all worthwhile. By midnight, I have to accept that Ally is a no-show. As I can barely keep my eyes open, I lock up my maisonette and haul myself upstairs.

I live in south London. It's a nice area near Battersea Park, and I did well to find this little maisonette, stretching my finances at the time, but it was definitely worth it. The value of properties around here continue to skyrocket. I know I'm lucky to own my own home, however modest it is. It's a luxury so many of my generation haven't achieved, but then I paid a heavy emotional price for the privilege. I try not to dwell on it. After taking a quick shower, I flop into bed, stuff my foam earplugs into my ears and try to focus on my breathing rather than the heavy beat of the neighbour's music. It must work because I drift off into a deep sleep.

I'm startled awake by my phone ringing. Who the hell is calling me in the middle of the night? If it's a wrong number, they can expect a tirade of abuse. I fumble around and eventually find my phone just in time to see Rob's name on my mobile. Why is he calling me at 3 am? My finger hovers on the accept call button because I just know. I know that something terrible has happened.

'Rob,' I say breathlessly.

I can't understand a word he's saying. 'Rob, is that you?'

'She's gone, Simone!'

'What do you mean she's gone?' My voice is a hoarse whisper.

'Ally's dead. My beautiful wife is dead!' And then he's wailing, as if his heart has been sliced out of his body, and I can't understand another word he's saying. I hear another voice in the background. A woman. There are muffled noises and then a stranger's voice.

'Is this Simone Carver?'

'Yes.' The blood in my veins is pumping so loudly, it feels as if drumbeats are beating in my ears.

'I'm so sorry, Simone. My name is PC Deidre Withington, and I'm with your brother-in-law. I'm afraid your sister was killed in a car accident a few hours ago.'

'No,' I whisper. 'No, that's not possible.'

'Is there anyone there with you, Simone?'

'No. I'm coming.'

'Are you sure?' But I hang up on her because this can't be true. Ally was on set. She would have taken the train home and then the tube. Rob has the car. But then I wonder. Perhaps if she knew she was going to be working late, she took the car this morning. But she doesn't drive when she's really tired. She's sensible like that. Or maybe she was in a taxi. Why didn't I ask any questions? I'm shaking so much I can't even pull on my jeans. I let out a sob. This can't be happening. My beautiful sister, so full of life, on the cusp of greatness. No, they must have got it wrong. It'll be someone else with the same name, or perhaps it's one of the other actresses on the film.

Somehow, I get dressed in yesterday's clothes. I grab my handbag and hurry out of the flat and down the stairs, tumbling out onto the road, where all is silent. My breathing is ragged and my footsteps deafening as I run down the street and onto the main road. I get lucky. A black cab passes, its light illuminated. That's the advantage of living in London, the city that's never properly asleep. I wave my arm, and the cab comes to an abrupt stop to avoid running me over.

'You need to be more careful, love,' he says as I throw myself into the taxi.

'27b Carlisle Street. As quickly as possible, please.'

I bite my lip hard and have to lick away the blood. It's as if my brain has shut down on me while my body is shivering violently, a coldness so deep inside, I wonder if I'll ever get warm again.

There's a police car parked outside Ally's house. The lights aren't flashing, but it looks out of place on this leafy suburban street. I shove some cash at the driver and race out of the taxi, running up the steps to my sister's house. The door swings open before I can press the buzzer.

THE NEXT FEW hours pass in a daze. It's like I've stepped into some horrific alternative reality, living out my very worst fears. Rob's parents arrive at 8 am, ashen-faced, aged by a decade or so since I last saw them just three months ago. I feel the loss of our parents all over again as I realise that this couple is the closest I have to family, even though we're not related by blood. I have never seen a man so broken as Rob. It's as if he has shrunken in on himself, so much so that he can't even speak to little Carly. We haven't told her yet; Rob just doesn't have the strength or the words. I think his parents are going to try to explain. But how can you tell a four-year-old that her mummy is gone for ever? Will she really understand?

I hear the patter of her footsteps upstairs and her innocent high-pitched voice saying, 'Granny, what are you doing here?'

I can't listen to this conversation, so I head to the kitchen and boil the kettle to drown out the sound of voices.

A little before 9 am, I decide it's time for me to go home. Rob's mother is upstairs playing with Carly, and his father is sitting in silence with Rob in the living room. Not that I want to leave, but what can I do here? And then the doorbell rings. I walk down the narrow hallway, with the stairs rising to my right and a wall full of coats and clutter on my left, the detritus of my sister's young child. Ally used to keep the house so tidy, but since she's been working all hours, the place has morphed into a tip. I open the door to the two police officers who were here last night, DS Graham Foley and PC Deidre Withington.

'Can we come in?' DS Foley asks.

I realise that I've just been standing in the doorway staring at them, wondering how they survive on so little sleep, a strange thought considering the nightmare we're living in.

'Yes, sorry.' I stand to one side. I lead them into Ally and Rob's small living room, where Rob is still sitting on his favourite chair, rocking backwards and forwards, his eyes sore and red. He glances up at them, and I see a fleeting expression of hope. Perhaps they're here to tell us they made a mistake and that it wasn't Ally after all in that car wreck. Rob's father gets up and moves to stand in front of the window.

I motion for police officers to sit on the green sofa, and I take the upright chair next to the large television.

'We have some news for you,' DS Foley says. 'I'm afraid–'

Rob's shoulders sink. Of course it's not good news. 'We have identified the car that Ally was driving as belonging to Marigold Delucci, otherwise known as Goldie Delucci. We understand that she runs the production company where Ally has been working. We think drugs may have been involved, although this hasn't been confirmed yet.'

'What!' I exclaim in unison with Rob. 'No, that's not possible. My sister never did drugs. She hated them. She saw what they did to some of her actor friends, and she swore she'd never touch them.'

'No!' Rob says before burying his head in his hands.

'I'm very sorry,' PC Withington says.

'Obviously we'll be carrying out further investigations, but, Rob, we do need to know if this is something Ally did, to the best of your knowledge?' DS Foley asks.

Rob stares at them, disbelief in his eyes, and shakes his head. His voice is low and hoarse. 'Ally doesn't do drugs. Neither of us do.'

The police officers glance at each other, and from their expressions, it's obvious they don't believe Rob. But they're wrong. I know without a shadow of doubt that Ally wouldn't have taken drugs. The only possibility is she was drugged without her knowledge.

'Was anyone else involved?' I ask, wondering why I didn't ask that last night.

'No. Ally was alone in the car.'

'Did she suffer?' Rob's voice cracks.

'There'll be an autopsy,' DS Foley says. 'We'll know more then. But hopefully not.'

'Why was she driving their car?' I ask.

'We'll be investigating that,' DS Foley explains. The police officers stand up. 'We'll be in touch when we have further information. Once again, we're very sorry for your loss. We'll see ourselves out.'

'Who are those people, and where is Mummy?' Carly is standing in the doorway to the living room, clutching her favourite rabbit toy, her T-shirt on the wrong way around. I look at this adorable little girl with her blonde mussed-up hair and a face just like her mother's and realise that it's up to me now. I will have to become her pseudo mother.

2

GOLDIE

We have a sophisticated doorbell that rings throughout the house and flashes up video images on my phone. I glance at it. There's a couple standing at the door. My first thought is that they're Jehovah's Witnesses. I've got nothing against them, but I really haven't got time to be politely ushering them away. I glance again. Perhaps not. It's the way they stand authoritatively, their legs planted apart, their eyes narrowed. God. If they're not Jehovah's Witnesses, are they police? What's Rose done this time?

I save my document, shove the laptop further along my glass desk and get up, slipping my bare feet into fluffy slip-ons and pulling my long, fawn-coloured cashmere cardigan tightly around me. They ring the doorbell again.

'Coming!' I say, although my voice won't carry through our well-insulated house. I hurry into the huge atrium that is our front hall and open the door. Minnie, our little white fluffball of a dog, barks, and I scoop her up into my arms to stop her from running outside.

'How can I help?' I ask, trying to be polite despite the

amount of work I have and the beginnings of a thumping headache. Please not another migraine.

'Are you Marigold Delucci?'

I grimace at the use of my given name. What the hell were my parents thinking giving me such a ghastly old-fashioned name? Mum said I was their flower, but the kids at school used to call me Rubber Gloves after the well-known kitchen washing-up gloves brand. It's no surprise I only use the name Goldie.

'Yes,' I reply cautiously.

'I'm DS Graham Foley, and this is my colleague PC Deidre Withington.' They flash their badges at me.

'What's this about?'

'Can we come in?'

'Are the kids okay, and Braun?' As far as I'm aware, both Rose and Florian are upstairs asleep.

'It's not about a member of your family,' DS Foley replies.

I let my shoulders sink and hold the door open. Deirdre Withington's eyes widen as she glances around the hall, like most people's do. This is an impressive house and frankly beyond my wildest dreams. We've done well for ourselves, Braun and I. At least that's the story I tell myself.

'Would you like a tea or coffee?' I ask, leading them into the kitchen. Their shoes squeak on the white marble floor.

'No, thanks,' they say in unison.

I'm glad. Hopefully that means they'll be out of here quickly. I can't imagine what it is they want from me. The kitchen is huge, with a five-metre island and smooth, pale grey units that create one continuous line down the length of the room. At the far end the slimline, sliding patio doors retract into each other so that the whole width of the room can open up to the garden beyond. I like the functionality of the room and that all the normal detritus of cooking can be hidden away.

'Have a seat.' I sit down at the smooth concrete table that was cast on site and cost the price of a small car.

'Can you confirm that you're the registered owner of a Porsche Cayenne, with a personalised registration number DLCC1?'

'Yes, why?'

'I'm afraid that your vehicle was involved in a serious accident last night.'

'What?' I exclaim. 'I didn't even drive it yesterday. Braun took it to the set, but it wasn't used during the day. I thought he'd left it at the studios.'

'Braun being Mr Delucci, your husband?' DS Foley asks.

'Yes. Was someone hurt?' My heart is thumping now. Was the car stolen? I thought it was still in the studio car park at the industrial estate where we've been filming for the past few weeks.

'I'm sorry to tell you that a woman called Alison Greystone passed away at the scene.'

I feel shock reverberate through me. I stand up and pace the kitchen. 'Ally? What was Ally doing driving my car? She can't have died.'

'I realise this is a great shock. We understand she was one of your actresses. Is that right?'

'Yes.' I run my hand through my hair. What the hell are we going to do? Ally is dead. It doesn't make sense.

'Is your husband at home? Because we need to speak to him too.'

I shake my head. 'No, he's in the editing suite. He was there until late last night and has been out since first thing this morning. We're working to an incredibly tight deadline.'

'Can you give us your husband's phone number, please.'

'Sure.' I reel it off.

'Was anyone else hurt?' I ask.

'No one else was involved. I'm afraid your car is very

damaged, and we expect that once it's been released from our enquiries, it will be written off by your insurers. You will need to contact them.'

I sit down again.

'Did Ally regularly use your car?' DS Foley asks.

'No, never. Only Braun and me drive it. Did she steal it?' That doesn't make any sense. Ally is a sweet young woman, innocuous even, except when she's in character, and then she really comes alive. Except if what the police say is true, she isn't alive and never will be again. I stuff my fist against my mouth. This is too terrible.

'Are you suggesting that your car was taken without your or your husband's permission?'

'I can't be sure that Braun didn't let her drive it, but it's not like it's a company car. Anyone is insured to use it, but it's normally only Braun and me.'

The police officers stand up, and I see them out.

'We may need to speak to you again,' DS Foley says.

I CALL BRAUN IMMEDIATELY.

'We're right in the middle—' he says.

I interrupt him. 'Ally's dead.'

'What?'

'Ally crashed my car and was killed last night.'

Braun gasps. 'Holy shit. That's terrible.'

'What was she doing driving my car?'

'I've no idea. I can't believe it.'

'But you had my car yesterday. Didn't you authorise her to use it?' Braun's car, a red E-Type Jaguar, his pride and joy, is in the garage yet again.

'No, of course not. After we wrapped and you left with Gina, the cast and crew got out the beers. I wanted to see what yesterday's filming was like, so Martin and I headed back to the editing suite. We were there for a couple of hours, and then I came home.'

'But how did you get home? Why didn't you take my car?'

'I'd had a couple of beers with the cast, you know what it's like. Martin offered to drive to the editing suite, and then I got a cab back home. I left your car on set. Shit. I can't believe Ally took it. It's not like her to do something like that.'

'Where did you leave the car keys, anyway?'

'In my jacket pocket where I always do.'

There's some shuffling in the background. 'They're not there.'

'Obviously they're not; how else could Ally have taken the car?' I can't stop the overtone of frustration in my voice. Sometimes Braun is so thick.

'What are we going to do?' Braun asks.

'I don't know. I'll get Lauren to ring the insurers and get us a courtesy car. Apparently mine is a write-off.'

'How's it going to affect the filming?' Braun asks the question I can't answer. I feel terrible for thinking this, but I wonder if it'll increase publicity for the film now that one of our leading actresses is dead or whether it'll create a dark cloud over the new release. This is so far out of my comfort zone.

'We'll have to tell everyone,' Braun says.

I sigh. 'Leave it with me.' Braun isn't known for his tact, and I'll need to take advice from the police on what I can or can't say. It's truly terrible. Ally was such a sweet little thing. Waif-like, very talented but much too serious and pure for an industry like ours. Nevertheless, this could have been her big break. If our film, *The Insomniac*, performs well at the box office as we expect it to, Ally would have been catapulted to the big time. Who knows, Hollywood might have come calling.

. . .

I GLANCE AT THE CLOCK. Where the hell is Lauren? She's our concierge, which is a stupid title, but one the recruitment agency insisted upon. Apparently it's more prestigious than personal assistant, which is what she really is. Lauren manages things at home for us, doing our admin, making sure the bills get paid and the kids' school forms get completed. And at times like now, during the school half-terms and holidays, she takes the children to and from their various holiday clubs. She's a housekeeper-cum-nanny really. Even though she's not great at her job, I couldn't manage without her at the moment. She lives in our basement flat. It has a separate entrance, a little kitchenette, living room, bedroom and bathroom. A very nice perk of the job.

I'm inundated, trying to wrap up this film and get funding for the next one. Braun and I run Delucci Productions. He's the director, and I'm the producer, which basically means my husband is the artistic talent, and I'm the business brains. We may be fifty per cent shareholders, but there wouldn't be a business if it weren't for me. I'm the one who juggles every-thing, and I mean everything.

Poor Ally. And her poor family. I think she's got a young child too. My jumbled thoughts are interrupted by my mobile ringing. Lauren's name flashes up.

'I was just wondering where you were,' I say. 'About to come down and find you.'

'Sorry, Goldie, but I don't think I can work today. I've been throwing up most of the night. Sorry I didn't message you earlier, but I fell back to sleep.'

'Oh,' I say, and then remember that I need to be sympa-thetic. 'Hope you feel better soon.'

'Thanks. And I hope I haven't passed the sickness bug on to any of you.'

That would just about break me. Braun and I cannot afford to be ill. What a bloody awful morning.

'I'll need to use your car for the next few days.' I decide not to explain why to Lauren. I'll deal with the insurance company myself. The white electric Volkswagen is another perk of her job; she uses it to ferry the children around and do the shopping. And it eases the conscience a little having a fully electric car when Braun in particular drives a gas guzzler.

'What's for breakfast?' Our thirteen-year-old son, Florian, shuffles into the kitchen. He's a small boy in comparison to his classmates. Braun was a late developer too, apparently, and now look at him. He's six feet, broad chested with a strong jaw, my tall, dark, and handsome husband.

'You'll have to make it for yourself. Having a bad morning.'

'I don't know how to do eggs and bacon,' Florian whines.

'Have some toast instead. Oh, and you're going to have to go to football camp every day until Lauren is better. She's ill.'

'No.'

'Sorry, love, but Lauren is off sick, and I've got too much work to do to babysit you.'

'But you said I didn't have to go.' Florian looks like such a little boy now with his trembling lower lip. 'I can't go. It's not fair, Mum.'

'I'm sure you'll enjoy it more than you think you will. Half your classmates will be attending. It'll be fun.'

'I'm not going. I'll just stay here alone.'

'No you will not, young man.'

'Rose can look after me.'

'No bloody way,' seventeen-year-old Rose says as she saunters into the kitchen wearing an oversized black T-shirt and black Doc Martens. Her white legs are goose-pimpled and skinny. Her hair is dyed a dark black, much too dense a colour against her pale face, and is cropped short and spikey. She has multiple piercings in her ears and, to my disgust, piercings in her nose and tongue. We had an almighty row when she came home with those, but I've just had to accept that she's going through her goth stage. I suppose it could be much worse.

'Actually, Rose, it would be helpful if you could be here this afternoon when Florian gets back from camp.'

'No can do.'

'I'm not asking, I'm telling you. You need to be back here for 4 pm.'

'But I'm busy.'

Florian darts out of the kitchen. 'Where are you going?' I shout after him.

'I'm not going to camp, and you can't make me.'

'You're such a bitch, Mum. Can't you see that he doesn't want to go? He's crap at sport, and all the other boys will take the piss out of him.'

'Don't talk to me like that!' I say. Rose rolls her eyes at me and turns the water tap on. I realise that I have no control over my children, but the reality is, they've had to play second fiddle to this film. If they expect us to pay for their private education and to give them the lives of luxury they've become so used to, then that's the sacrifice we all have to make. Rose has become rather feral, and Florian has withdrawn into himself, but I simply don't have the time to give them as much focus as they need. I feel bad about it, of course I do. I'm their mum, and I love them. It's a fallacy that women can do it because I'm permanently riddled with guilt. When I was Rose's age, I was working two jobs: full time in Dorothy Perkins and evenings in the local pub. I didn't have anyone to pay my way. I'd promised myself I'd give my children a much better childhood than I had, and in many ways, that's what I've done.

Rose gulps a glass of water down in one, slams the glass

into the sink and walks out of the kitchen. She's incapable of putting anything directly into the dishwasher.

'Where are you going?'

'Out,' she says, over her shoulder.

It's a losing battle. My head thrums, and I realise there's nothing I can do. 'Just keep out of trouble,' I say, but the front door slams closed, and even if she heard me, I know she won't pay me the slightest bit of attention. Rose is trouble. In fact, she's a total nightmare. Is it okay to say that about one's own child? These days, I barely recognise her.

3

ROSE

I hate my parents. Mum acts all sanctimonious, thinking she can tell me what I can and can't do, but I'm an adult now, and there's nothing she can do to stop me. Dad acts like he's some superstar. I mean honestly, his head is so far up his backside it would be funny if it wasn't so tragic. They think they're super cool A-listers, when the reality is not a single celebrity or film star has ever visited our house. Me and my mates have never heard of any of the actors they've cast in their films, so obviously they're nobodies. But Delucci Productions is all Mum and Dad talk about; it's all they care about. I don't even know why they bothered having children because they're never there for Florian and me. They just farm us out to school and holiday clubs and stupid Lauren. Sometimes it really gets to me, like this morning. Doesn't Mum get how shitty it is for Florian? It's bloody obvious that he's gay, yet Mum insists that he goes to football camp and be all fake macho like Dad. At least I'm old enough to do my own thing. Thank goodness we live in London, and I can get out, meet up with my mates, hang around and keep myself busy. It's harder for him, being four years younger. Not that

I'd ever tell him I feel sorry for him, but I do. I know he's bullied at school and struggles with schoolwork. I tell him not to bother, like me, but he takes everything so seriously. I stride down the street with my rucksack bouncing on my back. The sun's shining, which is perfect because the tourists will be out. I head for Putney Bridge Station and jump on a District Line tube towards Victoria. I've got high hopes for today. I put my earbuds in and turn the music up loud and relax into the seat. Mum thinks I'm lazy and thick. Just because I flunked my GCSEs doesn't mean anything. School bores me, so of course I wasn't going to 'apply' myself. My talents lie elsewhere.

I started shoplifting a couple of years ago. My mate Charlie dared me to nick some lipstick at Selfridges of all places. I mean, it's not somewhere I'd ordinarily go, and not only that, she wanted me to steal the most expensive lipstick in the shop. We're talking a fifty-quid lippy. Ridiculous. That day, I took one of Mum's jackets, caked on the make-up and made myself look at least three years older. Not only did I steal the lipstick without being caught, I also took some mascara and a perfume. Charlie was seriously impressed. The thing is, it's all about confidence. If you walk into a place as if you own it, then people think you do. But shoplifting isn't thrilling anymore. I can steal pretty much anything, but there's not much I want. It's ironic, because Mum and Dad are the most materialistic people I know, but who needs stuff? No, it's all about experiences for me, and shoplifting no longer gives me the buzz and just isn't worth the hassle.

I found this website dedicated to scammers. It's seriously cool and shares some brilliant ideas. I spent the summer holidays trying them out, and one of the best is being a waitress. It's hilarious really, because Mum said I should get a holiday job, and she suggested I apply to be a waitress. I mean why would I want to do that for real?

At Victoria Station, I swap onto the Victoria Line and head to Oxford Circus. The tube is heaving now, mainly full of tourists and day trippers. It would be too cheugy to pickpocket these idiots who walk around with their wallets in their pockets and their handbags unzipped. No, I intend to try out my latest scam. It's a laugh and a half. Oh, if you're not a Gen Z like me, and don't know what it means, cheugy is basic or ordinary.

I walk along Oxford Street, dodging the dawdling shoppers, and then head up towards St Christopher's Place. There are lots of restaurants there, most of which have seating outside. Perfect. I hide in the shadows of a doorway for a while, checking out which restaurants have the most customers and the least staff. Then I pull a black apron out of my rucksack, tying it around my waist. I leave the rucksack behind a dumpster bin. There's nothing in it worth nicking. I put my house key, phone and wallet in the apron pocket, take a few deep breaths and plaster a smile on my face, then stride up along the pavement and into the seating area. I grab a menu that's been discarded on an empty table. A couple are just sitting down. They look Middle Eastern and rich. He's wearing a flashy gold Rolex, and she's got bright yellow gold rings on every finger and hair that's luxuriantly long and bouffant.

'Good morning, sir, madam,' I say, handing the menu to the man. 'Are you here for an early lunch or just drinks?'

'We'd like something to eat,' he says, giving me a creepy smile.

'Fabulous. Now, because you're sitting outside, I'm afraid we have to ask for your credit card to secure your order.'

'Oh,' he says, frowning slightly.

I lower my voice. 'We have so many people who just get up and walk out. It's terrible,' I say, with a grimace. 'I wish we didn't have to be mistrustful, but it's the restaurant's policy. If you'd rather sit inside, then of course it's different in there.'

'No, it's no problem,' the man says, pulling his soft leather wallet out of his designer jeans' pocket. He pulls out a platinum American Express card.

'Oh dear, I'm so sorry. We don't take Amex. Do you have a MasterCard or Visa?' I ask.

'Sure.' He hands me a black MasterCard.

'Thank you, sir. I'll be back in just a tick to take your order.'

The next few seconds are the most dangerous. If I walk into the restaurant and I'm seen by another member of staff, then the whole scam could fall apart, so it's one hell of a risk. My heart is pumping, and I can feel blood rushing to my cheeks. But the adrenaline is all part of the fun. I stride with purpose into the doorway and stand just inside. No one is there. I quickly untie my apron and shove it behind the door. I've got a stash of them, and it's safer to leave it behind. Then, when a waitress ambles out onto the terrace, I walk behind her and, without a backwards glance, stride straight out onto the street, turning right and walking with my shoulders back towards the dumpster bins and out of sight.

When I'm around the corner, I glance over my shoulder. No one is following me. The couple are deep in conversation, their heads almost touching. How nauseatingly sweet. I wonder what they'll think when they realise their credit card is gone. I need to scarper.

I'M NOT INVINCIBLE. Only stupid people think they are. They're the types who get overly confident and then make mistakes. You need to swap it up, do different things, to challenge yourself. I screwed up last month. I found some instructions on YouTube on how to break into a vehicle and start it. I haven't even passed my test, so I probably wouldn't have nicked the thing, I just wanted to prove that I could do it. I chose an old, knackered-looking car, a couple of streets around the corner from us at home. Not easy to find because the streets of Putney are mostly lined with fancy Teslas and rechargeable cars that are laden with electronics. Anyway, it was after dark, and I was struggling to get the door open. I got too engrossed in following the video on my phone, and I got nicked. It was a couple of police officers who just happened to be cruising past. They hauled me off to the police station, although I'm not sure they could really have arrested me because I hadn't actually broken into the car. I gave them Dad's number, and when he turned up to get me, he thought it was hilarious. The police let me off with a warning because I didn't have any previous, and I showed them the video on YouTube and said I'd just wanted to prove I could do it. I think secretly, they were quite impressed. It's just a shame I didn't actually open the door. Anyway, Dad promised not to tell Mum, and so far he's kept his promise. He told me that he did some stupid stuff when he was my age, and look where he is now. I would have told him he was just some second-rate director, except I needed to keep him onside, so I bit my tongue.

I take out the MasterCard and have a look at it. J. Abadi. That's good. If it had a full name on it, like an obviously male name, then I might have to dump it, but I can be J. Abadi for the afternoon. I head for Covent Garden and the market shops. There's not much I want, really. A new denim jacket perhaps or some nice-smelling soap. I choose shops that sell cheap things and only spend less than a hundred quid at a time, making sure I'm safely within the contactless limit. Obviously I try to avoid CCTV too, although I'm not too bothered about that. I buy Florian a book on how to draw anime cartoons. Of course he can get stuff off the internet, but I think he'll like it. I sit for a while, drinking a milkshake and smoking a few cigarettes. It's nice out here, where I know no one and no one knows me. I feel free. When the sun goes down, I saunter back towards the tube station. Passing a Costa Coffee, I nip inside, buy a sandwich, a muffin and a large cup of coffee to go. Balancing them all, I walk outside. There's a homeless guy sitting on the pavement just outside the tube station. I got chatting to him a few weeks back, and his story broke my heart. His girlfriend chucked him out, and he got in with some wrong people, got hooked on drugs, and one thing led to another. It could happen to any of us.

'Hey, Joe,' I say. 'Got you a few bits and pieces.' I hand him the food and drink from Costa and pull out a thick jumper from my rucksack, tearing the price label off it. At sixty quid it's the most expensive thing I've bought this afternoon. 'Thought you could do with this now the nights are getting colder.'

'You're an angel, you know that, right?' he says. He swipes his eyes before reaching up for the jumper. I bite my lip because it's embarrassing to make a grown man cry.

'Yeah, well. Just doing my bit,' I say awkwardly. 'I'll be seeing you then, Joe.' I give him a little wave as I walk away.

'God bless,' he shouts after me.

There's a rubbish bin a bit further down, and I hurry towards it, dropping J. Abadi's credit card into it. He got lucky, really. I only spent just over a hundred quid in total, and I'm sure J. Abadi with his Rolex and everything won't miss the cash.

You see, that's what gives me a buzz. Stealing from the rich to give to the poor.

4

SIMONE

The last few weeks have been hell. Pure hell. Ally's accident doesn't make any more sense to me today than it did the night it happened. My sister didn't do drugs. She didn't just take people's cars without their permission. She thought the Deluccis were gods because they gave her a big break. There's just no way she would have stolen Goldie's vehicle, not unless she was put into an untenable situation. But no one is listening to me.

I can't really blame the police. They've been as helpful as they can be, and the coroner did his job, but I know in my heart of hearts that they've got it all wrong. Rob agrees with me, but he's so broken he can't even string a proper sentence together.

Apparently methamphetamine was found in Ally's bloodstream. A needle mark in her arm. Had things got so stressful that she'd resorted to taking hard drugs? I know absolutely nothing about the film industry, but is it de rigueur to do drugs? Surely not. Things have changed for the better since #metoo – even Ally said so herself.

I've had lots of conversations with Deirdre Withington

over the past weeks. With her straight brown hair cut short and rectangular glasses, she's a no-nonsense type of woman and the only one prepared to listen to me spout my theories. Apparently Goldie and Braun very occasionally got people to park her car or use it for errands. That's Goldie's car because no one was allowed to even go near Braun's E-Type Jaguar. And the keys were left lying around on set, in Braun's jacket pocket or on a side table. It sounds like security was pretty lackadaisical. I've told Deidre until I'm blue in the face that Ally didn't do drugs. I even wrote to the coroner. But the inquest verdict has come back as death from a road traffic collision as a result of being under the influence of drugs. Deidre says they have investigated properly and that the facts are the facts. Ally had meth in her system, and she drove the car, at a crazily high speed, into an old oak tree. The tree won.

And so I'm meant to put all of that behind me, to move on, to grieve and be a mother figure for little Carly. It sounds so easy, doesn't it? Grief is never a linear process and especially when the events surrounding the death are so suspicious. I don't believe the police, and I don't believe the coroner, and most of all I don't believe the Deluccis.

To compound Rob's misery and mine, there has been a lot of media interest surrounding Ally's death, and I wouldn't be surprised if the Deluccis have been stoking it up. The headlines screamed, 'Tragic loss of rising superstar actress'. It's as if they're using Ally's death to promote their new film, and it sickens me. We had a private funeral, just Rob and his family, me and a handful of Ally's closest friends, but I really thought I would have had a request from the Deluccis to attend. After all, if she hadn't been working for them at an ungodly hour and they hadn't put such pressure on her, my sister would never have been driving their car and would certainly never have had drugs in her body. But no. Other than a handwritten note from Goldie a couple of days after Ally's death, Rob and I have had no contact with them.

I decided to lie low. I don't want my face in the papers as the sister of the actress who died. But most of all, I want to lie low so that I can uncover the truth. As each day passes, I become increasingly suspicious that events were not as the police described them. Deirdre Withington told me that everyone has solid alibis for the evening of Ally's death. Unsurprisingly, I suppose. Apparently, the vast majority of the cast and crew were still on set, drinking beer and celebrating the end of shooting the film. Goldie was at home on a Zoom call with some potential investors in Los Angeles, trying to raise funds for her next project, while Braun was in the editing suite that night, well into the early hours, apparently. If Ally hadn't been driving Goldie's car without the Deluccis' permission, then perhaps I would believe them. If she hadn't had drugs in her system, then perhaps I would believe them. But the two just don't add up. I know my sister better than anyone in the world, and I know deep in my gut that the Deluccis had something to do with her death. I'm determined to find evidence to prove that. Quite how, I've no idea.

ROB AND ALLY fell in love so quickly, and if I'm being honest, I wasn't sure whether the relationship would work. Yet it seems I was wrong. They adored each other, and when Carly was born, I think they had the perfect little family. Rob works in advertising. He's got a good job as the creative director of a medium-sized firm and earns enough so Ally didn't need to contribute financially. The only thing missing was the fulfilment of Ally's acting ambitions. And then about a year ago, she went for an audition with Delucci Productions, and it seemed like her dreams were about to come true. Yet the weeks in the lead-up to her death were not all rosy. She didn't talk about what was going on, but her face and body revealed the stress she was under. There are other things that don't add up. How did Braun get home that night, or did he go home at all? The police won't share that little nugget with me. All Deidre Withington said was there was no suggestion of criminal or suspicious behaviour. So why was Ally driving Goldie's car? And where was she going? Was she heading home or somewhere else? Everyone has drawn a blank on that one.

I've tried to concentrate on work, and I even went out on a date. That was a total waste of time. I have to accept that I won't rest easy until I have some answers, and that means finding out more about the Deluccis. Perhaps Leila, Ally's best friend, might know more. They met at school and pursued their acting dreams together, attending drama college and sharing a cheap bedsit in a grotty basement in Finsbury Park. Success came faster for Leila. Focusing on musical theatre, she's been in numerous productions both in the West End and in a show that made it to Broadway.

I call her. 'I'm sorry I didn't get to speak to you properly at Ally's funeral,' I say.

'I totally understand,' Leila says. 'We were all too choked up. Still are. How are you coping, Simone?'

'As well as can be expected. I can't believe she's gone.'

'None of us can. It's such a tragedy, and I miss her so much,' Leila says. Her voice cracks a little.

'I wanted to ask you, Leila, when did you last see Ally?'

She sighs. 'I'll never forgive myself for not pushing to see her. Three, four months even before the accident. She was so busy. To think we used to see each other twice a week at least. I don't suppose Carly would even recognise me now, and I'm her godmother.'

'Don't beat yourself up,' I say. 'Did you and Ally have any mutual friends who were also involved in the Deluccis' film?'

'Only Kit. Why?'

'I'd love to talk to some of the people who worked with her, just find out Ally's state of mind, what things were like for her during the last few days.'

Leila sighs. 'It doesn't feel real, does it?'

'Nope.'

'I'm due to meet up with George, Kit and some of my and Ally's friends on Wednesday evening. Kit and Ally have known each other a long time. Why don't you join us?'

'If you're sure.'

Leila gives me the name of the pub and time.

'You won't say anything, will you?' I ask. 'I don't want anyone to think I'm prying. I just want to feel closer to her.'

'Don't worry, Simone. I know exactly how you feel. I miss her so much.'

I KNOW there are plenty of sisters who are close, but Ally and I were more than close. We were bonded through grief. Our ordinary, happy family came to a shattering end when I was sixteen and Ally was fourteen. Dad dropped dead from a heart attack. He was at work and died in the post room. How ignominious. I told Ally that Mum died of grief. She took her own life by taking an overdose of painkillers just five months later. For years I've questioned why Ally and I weren't enough for her, but we clearly weren't. She and Dad had been a couple since they were kids, and she just couldn't live without him. At least she chose to die by suicide when Ally and I were away staying with our cousins in Worthing. It was her sister, my poor aunt, who found her. When, after three days, Mum hadn't rung to speak to us, Aunty Carla had a feeling something was seriously wrong. She called the police, but Mum had already been dead for two days. So that left me and Ally all alone, so I stepped into the role of parent. I don't think I've ever fully disengaged. I even gave Ally away when she got married.

Wednesday evening comes around quickly, and I find myself in a dank, beer-scented pub in Camden. Leila introduces me as Ally's sister and her friend. I recognise a couple of people from Ally's parties. We all sit around a group of tables wedged together, nursing glasses of wine and beer. I engineer it so I'm next to Kit.

'What's it like working for the Deluccis?' I ask, trying to sound as casual as possible.

'Yeah, alright.' And then it's as if he changes his mind. 'Honestly, they're just very pleased with themselves, Braun particularly. He saunters around as if he's some cool dude with a unique artistic vision, but he's just a bit of a prat. Goldie seems nicer, but she wasn't on set much. They made us work the most crazy hours. I've never been in a film where we had to work such long hours, and believe me, I've worked some ridiculous hours. There was a woman who used to tip up with them from time to time, their concierge.' He air marks the word with his fingers. 'She'd bring them fancy sandwiches and stuff while the rest of us had to make do with the catering, which was always crap. If anyone had a non-artistic question, we had to go through her.'

'What's a concierge?' I ask, sipping my white wine. 'Thought that was someone who worked in a hotel and arranged theatre visits and stuff for guests.'

'She was like a live-in assistant, I think. Someone who manages their home lives, diaries and the like. I'm not really that sure. All I know is that no one could get Braun to commit to a thing without it going through Lauren.'

'Were you there on the last day of filming?'

'You mean the night Ally died?' He sighs.

I nod, my fingers gripping the stem of the glass too tightly.

'Nah. I only had a bit part, not like Ally. I wasn't on set at all during that final week of filming.'

'What are you doing now?' I ask, just to be polite because if he wasn't there that night, then Kit can't help me.

'Things are looking up for me. I've got a role in a play at Chichester theatre, so I won't be in London much over the next few months.'

Just then a young man comes over and sits on Kit's lap. Kit introduces him as his boyfriend, and as they clearly only have eyes for each other, I take the opportunity to slip away. An idea is forming, a way to find out some more.

You might have thought it would be difficult to discover where the Deluccis live, considering they're reasonably high profile. Not so. They have registered their company, Delucci Productions, at their home address in Putney, so a quick search of the register at Companies House gives me all the details I need. Late the next afternoon, I take the 337 bus to Putney, and just thirty minutes later, I'm standing outside the Deluccis' house.

It is ridiculous. How can anyone afford a place this big in this part of London? It's a wide, white house, double fronted with its own drive and off-road parking. To the left of the house is a large beech tree. It looks a bit out of place in this urban landscape. I sit on a low wall on the opposite side of the street, periodically looking at my watch and phone, as if I'm waiting for someone. I hope I'm not picked up on any covert CCTV because this isn't the sort of place one can hang around and go unnoticed. I glance at my watch. It's 6 pm and dark, I've no idea if this Lauren is working today or what time she finishes, but I assume if she's live-in, she's not doing nine to five hours. I've wrapped up warmly in a thick coat and decide to hang around until 7.30 pm, and if I don't see anyone by then, I'll call it a day.

At 6.45 pm, a side door opens, and a woman, probably mid to late twenties, comes out. She's wearing leggings and a sweatshirt, a blue crossbody bag slung over her front. Her chestnut-brown hair is tied back in a ponytail, and she has a fringe that drops down over her eyes. She bends down to tighten the laces on her trainers and then starts jogging gently. She's definitely not Goldie (whose pictures I've checked out online and on the Deluccis' website), but she could be a friend of the family. However, I get a gut feel that I've struck lucky. I follow her. Just three streets away, she enters a gym. I stand back and wait a few minutes. Taking a deep breath, I stride inside and walk up to the reception.

The young man glances up and smiles at me, his head tilted quizzically. 'Are you looking to join the gym?' he asks with an Australian accent. Goodness, are they that exclusive that he knows all the members?

'Oh no, sorry. Well, maybe. I'm actually here because my colleague, Lauren, left her water bottle at work, and according to her boss, she doesn't go anywhere without it. I was wondering if I could leave it for her.'

I dig into my bag and take out a silver water bottle. It's one I've had for a couple of years and is rather battered.

The receptionist takes it. 'Lauren who?' he asks. Okay, so they must have lots of members. Then I realise I'm not wearing gym clothes, so it's obvious I'm not here to exercise. I'm being dim.

It's not difficult to feign idiocy. 'Oh my goodness, I can't remember her surname. I'm so stupid. It's only day three in this job, and if I screw things up, my boss will fire me. Can you look her up? She'll have only got here about five minutes ago, max. Honestly, I don't know what the big deal is about the water bottle. It might be because Lauren's diabetic, and it's got some special medication in it.'

For a moment he looks dubious, and then seeing my pained expression, he shrugs and types something into his keyboard.

'Lauren Barton. Checked in four minutes ago.'

'Yes, silly me. That's her. Thank you so much. Would you mind giving her this?' I hand over the bottle, which is half-filled with water.

'Sure, no problem.'

'Thanks so much.' And then I skedaddle out of the gym. Now I have Lauren's name, hopefully I can track her on social media, and knowing where she works and the gym she visits, I intend to engineer a meeting.

5

GOLDIE

Braun and I are getting ready to have dinner with the directors of a film finance investment company. They're Americans on a whistle-stop tour of Europe, looking for financing opportunities for their uber wealthy private investors. I've been working to get a meeting with Todd Katz and Emma Garcia for months, and if we can persuade them that Delucci Productions is a solid investment potentially offering excellent returns, then our future will be secure.

'You look gorgeous,' I say to Braun as he straightens his tie. He's wearing a bespoke navy suit made by a Jermyn Street tailor that costs the earth, and we'll probably look ridiculously smart this evening, but better that than looking like slobs. 'Can you zip me up?'

Braun lifts my hair up and places a kiss at the back of my neck. 'Not looking so bad yourself, darling,' he says. I smile. I had my hair done this afternoon, my make-up is carefully applied, and now all I need to do is find my earrings. Striding into my dressing room, I never fail to admire the truly splendid bespoke carpentry on the cupboards and drawers with soft sliding mechanisms, frequently pinching myself that this is all mine. I open the black leather jewellery box, which I keep on top of the centre unit in the dressing room. There are just two items that I inherited from my beloved grandmother: the antique leather jewellery box and a pair of gold and pearl drop earrings. They're not particularly valuable, but they're my lucky earrings. I wore them on our wedding day, when we signed our first film and on every other significant day in my life, apart from when I gave birth to the kids. I'm not superstitious or naïve, but they give me confidence, and I'm sure going to need that tonight.

I lift up the lid and open the little drawer. It's empty. Did I put them in the wrong drawer by mistake? I pull open all the other little drawers and look in the body of the box. They're not there.

'Braun, have you seen my pearl earrings?' It's a futile question because Braun is the untidiest person I've met, and he certainly won't know where they are.

'Sorry, love,' he says as he walks out of the bedroom.

I try to recall when I last wore them. The reality is, the past few months have been so busy, I just can't remember. Perhaps they're in my bedside table. I dash back into the bedroom, my stockinged feet sinking into the pale grey deep-pile carpet, and pull open the drawer. I tip it out onto the bed and rummage through the strips of pills and tissues and earplugs. They're not there.

'We really need to get going,' Braun shouts from downstairs.

I glance at the clock. Our taxi will be here any moment. I curse as I rush back into the dressing room. I put in a pair of diamond earrings that Braun gave me for our tenth wedding anniversary. They're flashier, go better with my fitted black dress than the pearl ones would, but they're not what I want to be wearing. Rose. I bet Rose has them.

I slip my feet into my stiletto heels, grab my handbag and rush out of the bedroom and down the corridor to Rose's room. Despite her asking me repeatedly to knock on her door, I don't. She's lying on her stomach on the bed, over-ear headphones on, the curtains pulled, looking at something on her laptop. She slams the lid down when she realises I'm in the room.

'Did you take my granny's earrings? The pearl ones.'

She glowers at me. 'What would I want with those ugly old things?'

'I don't know where they've gone.'

'Don't blame me because you lose your stuff,' she says, turning away from me.

I grit my teeth. I don't have time for an argument. 'We're out for dinner. Lauren is here, and please stay in this evening.'

She grunts in response.

The doorbell rings as I hurry down the floating staircase and into the kitchen. Lauren is in there with Florian. I rush in and give him a quick kiss on the top of his head.

'Goodnight, darling. Are all the papers in my briefcase?' I ask Lauren.

'I printed off the emails as you asked,' she says.

'That's great, thanks. And my notebook, have you put that in the bag too?' I don't go anywhere without my pale blue Day Book. I have a large collection of them, all numbered so I don't get confused. I write down everything in them: all my ideas, my preparations for meetings, my to-do lists. My current Day Book is my bible.

'Sure thing.'

I grab my black crocodile leather bag, rush into the hallway and take my black cashmere coat off the hanger in the hidden cupboard. And then we're en route to central London.

. . .

I WAS right in thinking Braun and I would be overdressed. Todd Katz is in jeans, and Emma Garcia looks like she's wearing a brown paper bag. I doubt very much that it's California chic, and I imagine she'll be bitterly cold here in London. There's lots of air kisses and fake greetings, and then we sit down at a table set for four, covered in white linen and laid with sparkling silver cutlery.

'Well, it's great to meet you. I hear you're the production house in London to watch,' Todd says.

Braun laughs awkwardly. Considering that of the two of us, he's the one from the monied background, he should be used to these types of meetings, but he finds them difficult. I think he tries too hard. I find it easier to read people.

'So tell us about your next film, and perhaps you could answer the questions I emailed to you.'

'Sure,' I say, trying not to frown. What questions? What email? Perhaps they were on one of the emails that Lauren printed off. I might have to wing the answers, but I'm generally able to give off-the-cuff replies that sound knowledgeable. I open up my bag and take out the papers, rummaging for my notebook. It's not there. Surely Lauren didn't forget to put it in? I specifically asked her to take it off my desk and put it in my briefcase. Shit.

I flick through the pages of emails. There's nothing with a list of questions on.

'Ladies and gentlemen, what can I get you to eat?' I'm grateful for the waiter's interruption.

'So, back to my questions,' Todd Katz says once we've placed our orders.

'I'm afraid I don't seem to have that email,' I say with an easy smile that I hope doesn't reflect the churning of my stomach along with the mixture of nerves and annoyance.

Todd frowns, but then he starts firing detailed questions at me, asking for figures that I don't have, market research results on topics we haven't investigated, information on our competitors I have no knowledge about, and I come across as an amateur. Braun shuffles uncomfortably next to me, and I wish he'd come to my rescue, but that isn't Braun's thing. Yes, I have much of the information Todd is asking for, but it's not all committed to memory. How can I recall such detailed figures when I have so much else going on? By the time the main courses arrive, conversation has become stilted. It's obvious that the two Americans think they're wasting their time with us. No one orders a dessert, and we even forgo coffees. I think they're just eager to get out of here and away from us. Braun settles the bill, and Todd and Emma excuse themselves to take a phone call in Todd's hotel room. What an embarrassment.

'THAT WAS A BLOODY DISASTER,' I say, leaning my head back against the taxi seat.

'What happened?'

'Lauren didn't pack my Day Book. And she didn't print off the latest email from Todd, so I didn't have the information they were looking for.'

'Oh come on, you can hardly blame it on Lauren.'

'It's her job, Braun! If she'd done what I'd ask her to do, which, let's face it, is hardly difficult, then I would have had the information at my fingertips. I was prepared.'

Braun grunts. 'You seem to blame all of your mistakes on Lauren these days.'

'That's not fair! Lauren is screwing up left, right and centre. She's had lots of time off and failing to do the basics of what is required of her. I think she's going to have to go.'

'That's a bit of an overreaction, isn't it? You're just stressed and disappointed because this evening didn't go the way you wanted it to. These things happen, Goldie. There'll be other investors.' He squeezes my knee. 'Come on, love. There's no need to be so despondent. We've got time yet.'

Except that's where Braun is wrong. Our timeline is firmly committed to memory, and if we don't secure the bulk of the funding in the next four weeks, Delucci Productions might disappear into the ether.

I AWAKE with a start from a nightmare. My adorable grand-mother, who effectively brought me up because my parents were such useless layabouts, was standing in front of me, giving me a massive telling-off for losing her jewellery. She told me that my life would slip down the drain if I didn't find them. A silly dream, I know, but it still leaves my heart thumping and a layer of sweat over my body. I toss and turn for ages. It's as if the disappearance of my earrings resulted in the failure of the meeting, which I know is a ridiculous thought. Despite what Braun said, that meeting mattered, as do my earrings. I don't usually consider myself sentimental, but my grandmother was a wonderful woman, and to lose those earrings would be devastating. After a restless night, where I feel resentful towards Braun's easy sleep and relent-less snoring, I wave him off to the editing suite, and I tip the bedroom and dressing room upside down, looking in all my drawers, in the safe, in my handbags. I accused Rose of taking the earrings, but really, drop pearl earrings are just not her style. And then I think of Lauren. Would she have taken them? She might be inefficient, but a thief? Goodness, I hope not. I walk downstairs, through the utility room to the internal door that leads to her self-contained flat. I knock on the door, but there's no answer. I rarely go down here, because we gave her the space, and I feel it's only right to respect that. But now, I open the door and shout Lauren's name. There's no reply.

Damn it, I'm going to have a look. I pad down the narrow staircase and switch the light on in the basement hall. The room to the left is a small living room with a kitchenette, the bedroom is to the right. The door is slightly ajar, so I push it open further and switch the light on. There's limited daylight down here. The duvet is pulled up neatly and the wardrobe doors closed. I open them and run my fingers along her clothes. A silk scarf tumbles off a hanger. I bend down to pick it up and recognise it. It's an expensive Hermès scarf in black and white with pictures of dog collars. A weird design other than a dog collar featured in our first thriller film, *The Alsatian Files*. In the movie, the thieves hid their files on a USB stick, which they stashed inside the collar of their Alsatian dog. Braun's mother, Sylvia, gave me the scarf, and I thought it was a particularly thoughtful gift. There's just no way that Lauren would have a similar one. For starters, they cost over three hundred pounds. I rifle through the hangers and don't recognise any of my other clothes, but when I bend down and look through her shoes, there's a pair of black patent Jimmy Choo stilettos. I can't believe it. Not only is the woman useless at her job, she's a thief to boot.

I'm livid now, and I rummage through her belongings, pulling out the drawers of her bedside tables. I tug back the duvet and lift up the pillows. And gasp. Lying underneath her pillow are my grandmother's earrings. How could she do this to us? I feel utterly betrayed. I trusted this woman to live in our home, to look after my children, to manage our household accounts, to keep tabs on pretty much every element of our lives, and this is how she betrays me. Furiously, I rub tears from my eyes. Lauren is going to have to go. Today.

And then I hear a door opening upstairs and the creak of the stairs, footsteps coming downwards.

'Lauren,' I say as she swings open the door to the bedroom. She looks at me, and her mouth falls open.

'I know you've been struggling with elements of the job. You failed to put my notebook in my briefcase last night; you didn't print off all the emails as I'd asked, but you know, I could almost forgive that. But this–' I hold up the scarf with my left hand and open up the palm of my right hand to show the earrings. 'This is the ultimate betrayal.'

'I don't know what those are!' Her cheeks are flaming red, and she's sweating in her jogging clothes.

'They're mine, Lauren. Earrings I inherited from my grandmother, a scarf given to me by my mother-in-law and extremely expensive shoes. Were you going to sell them or just keep them for yourself? And what else have you stolen since you've been here?'

'It's not. I didn't... Where did you find those?'

'In your wardrobe and the earrings under your pillow.'

Her face flushes a deeper crimson. 'But I didn't put them there! I'd never steal from you or anyone. I'm an honest person, Goldie!'

'They just magically appeared in your room, did they?'

'They must have been planted in my room. Rose probably did it. She doesn't like me. Have you asked her if she put them here?'

'That really is stooping very low, Lauren. Accusing my daughter of setting you up. How dare you! You're fired for gross misconduct with immediate effect. I want you out of here tonight. And don't bother asking for a reference because I'm not going to give you one. I'm going to talk to the agency and tell them you're a liability and a thief.'

'But you're wrong, Goldie! I didn't do that. I wouldn't! You can't treat me like this.'

'Lauren, you're living in my house. Theft is a sackable offence, and as of now, you're fired.' I glance at my watch. 'You have eight hours to get out of my house, and if you don't go, then I shall be involving the police.'

Tears well up in her eyes. She opens and closes her mouth, but I don't hang around to discuss this any longer. Harsh as it is, I just want her gone.

6

ROSE

Mum and Dad won't pay for me to have driving lessons. I mean, how frigging unfair is that? All my friends are learning to drive. But Mum says I should get holiday and weekend jobs and earn some money to put towards it. It's not like they can't afford to pay for my lessons. What's even more crazy is I don't think I'll need many because I know how to drive already. I've done loads of sessions online, those driver awareness courses, and followed videos. So I decided to hell with them, and booked a test and paid for it myself. It's not like I need a job to get money. Duh. I can nick stuff, sell it on, and there's other ways I can get my hands on cash. My test date is in a fortnight, but even though I'm confident, I reckon it's probably a good idea to drive a real car beforehand. I'm going to take Mum's new one. Dad's E-Type is being mended again (I mean, when isn't it?), so he's got the car that Lauren used. Mum's is sitting in the garage next to the house, begging for an outing.

After her Cayenne was written off in that accident, she went and got herself an all-electric car. It's an automatic, and most of the time it's in the garage on charge. Today both

Mum and Dad are out – like, when aren't they? Poor Florian has been outsourced to some camp that no doubt he's hating, and I've told Mum that I'm attending a drama club thing that school has organised during the half-term holidays. She got all excited, saying that if I was interested in drama, she'd be able to find me lots of opportunities. No, thank you very much.

I go online and read through the car manual. It looks easy enough. Just start it by pressing the button, put the car into reverse, and off it'll go. There are only two pedals, the brake and accelerator, so how hard can that be? When I reckon I've absorbed enough, I go down to the garage, open the car up and take the charger out of the socket. Then I hop into the driver's seat. It's so empowering! I open the garage door by pressing on the remote control she keeps in the console, put my foot on the brake and put the gearstick into reverse. I press ever so gently on the accelerator, but this car is savage! It bolts backwards with just the gentlest touch. Shit, I nearly hit the wall. Okay, I need to take this a bit easy. I turn the steering wheel to the left, my foot barely pressing the pedal, but I get it a bit wrong, and the back of the car hits the hedge. I hope I haven't scratched anything because Mum will go mental. Alright, now onto the road.

This is so exciting! I AM DRIVING. Well, I'm going the speed of an old age pensioner, but who cares. This is happening! And then my phone rings. Fuck. It's Mum. I don't answer, but she rings again immediately.

I ignore it again. But she rings once more. And then it hits me. Does she know what I'm doing? Oh crap. I need to pull over, but I don't even know where the indicators are on this thing. I hit a button, and the windscreen wipers go berserk. A loud horn sounds from somewhere behind me, and my sweaty palms slip on the leather steering wheel. There's a space up ahead on the left, so I turn the steering wheel to the left and slow right down, but I overdo it and jerk the wheels up on the kerb. A cyclist is coming past, and I miss him by a whisper. He raises his fist at me at the same time as a white van driver keeps his hand on the horn. I stick a finger up to them all because it's not like I've hurt anyone. Mum rings for the fourth time.

'What is it?' I answer.

'Where are you?'

'At home.'

'And where is my car?'

'In the garage, I assume.'

'Do not lie to me, Rose!' Mum screams. 'Have you taken my car?'

I hesitate because how the hell is she even suspicious?

'Get out of the car. Lock it up and walk home. I'll be back in thirty minutes and don't you dare go anywhere other than home.' And then she hangs up on me. WTF? Mum never hangs up on me; it's normally the other way around. Has this car got a secret camera or something? Suddenly it doesn't seem a great idea to be inside it any longer, so I hop out, slam the door and lock it with the remote control, leaving it parked at an angle with the front tyre up on the pavement. The last thing I want to do is go home and face Mum's fury, but in the scheme of things, perhaps it's better that I do. I wonder if she'll get a parking ticket to boot. That would be quite funny.

Half an hour later, I hear the slamming of the front door. I brace myself.

'Rose, get down here now!' Mum shouts up the stairs. Her strident voice goes straight through me. It's not like she needs to shout. I saunter towards her, standing at the top of the stairs with my hands on my hips.

She is literally quivering, her face pure white except for the little spots of red on her cheeks, her lips flat and eyes narrowed. Well, this is quite the explosion.

'What the hell were you thinking?' Her voice is surprisingly quiet but so taut.

'How do you know, anyway?' I ask.

'Because the car has a tracker in it, and I get a notification on my phone when it's driven. And then there's the camera on the outside of the house.'

'You mean you're spying on me?'

'You stole my car, Rose.'

'It's not technically stealing, is it, because what's yours is mine and vice versa,' I say, quoting what Dad tells Mum from time to time.

'You haven't even passed your test! It's illegal, never mind the most reckless thing you've ever done. You could have killed someone, Rose. You don't know how to drive! You could have gone to prison for this. Did that ever cross your mind?'

'Firstly, I didn't kill anyone, and secondly, I do know how to drive, no thanks to you. I did perfectly well.' I chuck the key down the stairs, and even though my throw was perfectly accurate, she misses it, and it lands with a thud at her feet.

And then she screams. I mean really screams, at the top of her voice. 'Get to your room, now! You're a spoiled, irresponsible child, and you're not allowed out of the house for a fortnight. It's all about you, isn't it? I'll bloody lock you in if I have to!'

I hesitate, and then she hollers again, and I scarper.

'I hate you,' I mutter under my voice and slam my bedroom door shut.

I lie on my bed, my face down on my pillow, and sob. If Mum wasn't so tied up with all of her stuff, her work and all her kiss-ass actors, she might actually see me for who I am. It's not true that it's all about me; it's all about her. If she'd got me proper driving lessons, then I wouldn't have had to do this, for starters. There's a scratching at the door, which gets louder. Sniffing, I get up and open the door; Minnie comes bounding in. Thank goodness for Minnie. I scoop up our little white fluffball of a dog and bury my face in her soft fur. She licks my cheek, and I know that she's the only member of our family who is truly compassionate.

I DIDN'T REALISE there was a security camera on the outside of the house, but even so, I know I need to lie low for a few days. It's going to be a nightmare staying at home, but it's not like I'm short of stuff to do. First off is payback time for Mum. She's out again at some meeting that is oh-so very important. I saunter into her dressing room and rifle through her huge stash of clothes. I've never seen her wear half of this stuff, which is such a waste. She should be giving it to charity, supporting people like Joe who have nothing. I select a few items that I've never seen her wear. A couple of pairs of trousers, some sandals, three bags, four jumpers and a revolting candy pink blouse with a pussy bow. Next I find a fancy clothes hanger, one of those satin padded ones that she uses for her posh dresses. It takes a while to style the items. The trousers are the hardest, but I put them on the end of their bed, and then I photograph the whole lot. When I'm done, I put the stuff back in her dressing room and return to my room.

I set up a fake Facebook account and post all the items on Facebook marketplace. If this works, then I'll sell more of Mum and Dad's stuff, and if they complain, I'll tell them the money will be going to their charity of choice. That should make them think. If they don't miss them, then the cash will be for me. I'll give a bit to Joe and some of the other homeless people I see outside the tube stations. I think that's fair dos.

It takes a few boring hours, but I do get interest in all of the items, probably because they're designer gear, and I've priced them quite cheap. I check out the profiles of the people who've contacted me. A couple of them I discount because they look dodgy as hell, but there's one woman who seems loaded, and she buys the red handbag. It's annoying because I can't take the items I've sold to the post office, so I have to order some packaging materials online and get the postman to collect them in a couple of days. After faffing around sorting this for a while, I lie back on my bed and groan. This isn't a fraction of the fun I get from scamming in person. In fact, it's boring and lame. I want to be out there, pitting my wits against real people, looking them in the eye and getting away with it. I wish I had a partner in crime, someone I could do my scams with, someone I could really trust. That would be such fun.

After a couple of hours of mindless swiping on TikTok, I pace around the house, Minnie at my feet. I wonder where Dad keeps his stash. I know he takes stuff, things he shouldn't, things he keeps hidden from Mum. I smell it on him, and I can't believe Mum is so naïve not to realise. He chews peppermint gum after he's smoked, and sometimes, when he comes back late and tries – but fails – to tiptoe quietly around the house, his pupils are enlarged and dark. It's kind of sad that he has to get high at his age.

One of the many good things of Lauren not being here any longer is that no one is shadowing me as I wander around the house. I go into Dad's study, which is a small room off the hallway. There's a large computer screen that hums and shiny black cupboards and a chrome and black leather sofa. I pull out the drawers and rummage inside, but they're just full of papers. When I've checked everywhere, I lie down on the floor and lever myself under his desk. Bingo. He's taped a plastic bag to the bottom of his chair. That is pathetic. Honestly, I didn't think Dad would be so unimagina-tive to hide it there. I peel back the tape and remove the plastic bag, opening it up. It's only weed. Well, that's a disappointment. If there had been a few pills inside, I could have used them as bargaining chips. Got him to let me out of the house in return for not telling Mum, but with weed, I'm not sure she'll be that bothered. Might as well smoke it myself.

A FEW MINUTES LATER, I'm out in the garden, puffing on a spliff. It reminds me of Lauren. She found me smoking a cigarette a couple of weeks ago, and she went absolutely ballistic, telling me I'd get lung cancer and threatening to tell Dad. Just because she's a gym freak doesn't mean that everyone else had to be. Besides, it was none of her business telling me what I could or couldn't do, and frankly at that point, I'd had enough of her sanctimonious behaviour. I couldn't stand the woman. Who gave her the right to talk to me like that? I mean, she's not even old enough to be my mother, and she was employed as a secretary or something, not a nanny, although she told the world she was 'the Deluccis' concierge'. What a load of bollocks. Anyway, I told her to piss off, and she went scarlet in the face. It was hilarious because she actually didn't know how to reply to me. She opened and closed her mouth like a fish and then stormed off, no doubt to tell Dad. She fawned over Dad, thinking the sun shone out of his backside. Heaven knows why because he's just a disgusting old man who's trying way too hard to be young and cool. At least I got rid of Lauren. It was so easy to set her up for stealing, and Mum fell straight into my trap. There's not much Mum does these days that I like, but firing Lauren was seriously cool.

7

SIMONE

I followed Lauren Barton on a couple of occasions, but life has got in the way, and if I'm being honest, I'm not really sure what to say to her. I can hardly ask outright, did your employers have anything to do with my sister's death? Besides, she wouldn't know. I'm browsing LinkedIn, which I use to find new bookkeeping clients, and to my delight, I see that Lauren has changed her employment status. She's job hunting! Her last employment was 'Private Concierge for High-Profile Family', so that means she's left. I'm pondering what might have happened when the craziest of crazy ideas hits me. What if I try to get a job with the Deluccis? I bet I could do the concierge job with my eyes closed. It'll only be admin and the like. I could juggle some of my regular clients and palm off a few on some other self-employed bookkeepers I know, saying I'm off travelling for a month or so, and it's not like I wouldn't be paid, because I bet people like the Deluccis pay a decent salary. But am I too late? Could they have filled Lauren's vacancy already?

I pace my little office, which is the second bedroom in my maisonette. It's a bonkers idea, but the more I think about it, the more I reckon it's got legs. If I can work with the Deluccis, I can find out everything about them. I can discover whether Goldie or Braun allowed Ally to drive her car; what my sister's relationship was like with her producer and director. But first I need to find out more about the position, and that means getting to know Lauren. I can't put it off any longer. But how am I going to find her? I can't hang out at the gym all day every day in the hope she might show up.

I'm going to have to pretend to be a headhunter and contact her via LinkedIn. Firstly I buy a domain – www.AGBespokeProductions.co.uk and set up a one-page website. It's a bit crap, but I don't want to waste too much time on it. Then I set up a fake LinkedIn account using the new email from AGBespokePositions, just hoping that Lauren doesn't do too much probing and see that I've got no connections. Finally, I send her a message.

Dear Lauren,

I have set up a new business in the private concierge world. My first client is a very high-profile family with homes in Dubai, New York and London, and they're looking for an experienced personal assistant / concierge to fill a new vacancy. It's a six-figure salary. When I saw that you were job hunting, I thought you might be a suitable candidate. Would you be able to email me your CV, and if I think you're suitable, I'll arrange a time for us to meet.

Kind regards,

Sarah Connestra

I can't believe I'm doing this. I feel bad because this will surely get her hopes up, and I'm using her, but needs must. I remind myself that I'm doing this for Ally. Because how else am I ever going to find out the truth about what happened to my sister? Who put her in that car, and who gave her the drugs?

An hour later a message pings into my new email account.

Dear Sarah,

The job vacancy sounds very interesting. Please find attached my CV. I look forward to hearing from you.

Kind regards,

Lauren Barton

And now I have it: her home address and telephone number. I also can see the types of jobs she's done in her various roles, responsibilities for admin, ferrying children to and from school, managing household shopping and the like. There's nothing on the list that I couldn't manage myself. So next I need to engineer a meeting with her. I send her an email back an hour later suggesting we (as in Sarah Connestra, my alter ego) meet for a coffee and an interview in a Starbucks a couple of streets from where I live. She readily agrees. Now I just have to see if I can pull off my plan.

I arrive at the coffee shop a few minutes before the agreed time and set up my laptop at a table next to the window, as far from a table with wailing babies as possible. I'm wearing smart clothes, so I suppose I could be mistaken for a professional headhunter. Fortunately, other than the newbie mums with their offspring, the place is fairly empty. I just hope that when Lauren arrives, she'll choose a table near me. She's early. She glances around, obviously trying to work out if

Sarah is already here. I try not to glance up too often as she looks around the coffee shop, feeling her eyes on me. She strides over towards me.

'You're not Sarah, by any chance, are you?'

I look up with a startled expression. 'Um, no. I'm Simone.'

'Oh, sorry to disturb you. I'm meeting someone called Sarah, but I don't know what she looks like.' Lauren seems flustered now, and I feel a little sorry for her. She shuffles towards the counter and orders herself a coffee, which she carries to a table not too far away from me. I throw her a kindly smile, and she grins back.

It's hard not to watch her as she becomes increasingly nervous and impatient, biting her nails, constantly checking her watch and her phone. And then, after about twenty minutes, she dials a number. It's a wrong number, and I know because I chose it at random. At that moment, I put my laptop in my bag, but leave my notebook on the table. I get up and slowly walk past her just as she's muttering some profanities to herself.

'Looks like you're having as lousy a day as me,' I say casually.

She looks up with surprise. 'Yes. I've just been stood up by a headhunter.'

'Oh goodness. Let me buy you another coffee,' I say. 'We can share our woes.'

Lauren's eyes widen, and I wonder if for a moment she's going to decline, because it's weird, isn't it, being approached by a stranger like this. But then her face breaks into a smile.

'That's if you want to,' I say, pretending to backtrack. 'Sorry, I'm probably being much too forwards. It drives me mad sitting here alone all day, trying to concentrate.'

'Sure, that would be lovely.' She fumbles in her bag and takes out her wallet.

I wave it away. 'My treat,' I insist. 'For imposing on you.' It appeases my conscience a little when she eventually lets me buy her a latte. A couple of minutes later, I return carrying two cups of coffee. I place hers down at her table.

'Enjoy,' I say, hesitating as I stand next to her table.

'Sit down and join me if you have time.'

'Are you sure?'

'Of course. We can swap tales about our lousy mornings.'

I smile warmly, placing my coffee on her table and scooping up my belongings from my original table. With my back to her, I try to rearrange my expression. I'm a little shocked as to how good I am at this subterfuge lark. Perhaps it's not only Ally who was talented at acting. Maybe I also missed my vocation. Nevertheless, I do feel bad about conning Lauren. I turn around and stride towards her with a bright smile on my face.

'I'm Lauren, by the way,' she says as I sit down opposite her. She's much prettier close up, with a wide smile and pale blue, wide-set eyes. Her hair is loose today, falling in shiny, gentle waves onto the shoulders of her neatly ironed white shirt.

'And I'm Simone. Sorry for barging in on your morning.'

'Not at all. I got my hopes up, but it seems like I've been stood up.'

'Oh no, that's awful. What happened?'

'I'm job hunting and was contacted by someone on LinkedIn who had an interesting opportunity. I was meant to be meeting the woman here this morning, but she hasn't shown, and the mobile number she gave me doesn't work. I think it was a scam. It wouldn't surprise me if my ex-employers set it up.'

'Goodness, they don't sound like very nice people.'

'Oh, they're okay, I suppose. Their daughter is a handful, but the job wasn't really ideal. It was live-in for starters.'

'What do you do?' I lean towards her.

'I was a private concierge for a wealthy family. Goldie and Braun Delucci. You might have heard of them? They've got a film company.'

'Can't say I have, but I'm not really knowledgeable on the film world. Are they a bunch of luvvies?'

'Actually, no. Goldie is super stressed all the time, and Braun, well, he's lovely. Most of the time.'

'I've never even heard the job title private concierge before. What does it entail?'

'I did all their household admin, making sure the bills were paid, the shopping was in, the kids got to school, Minnie, their little dog, got fed and walked. I booked their holidays and did all the things normal people do, but wealthy and very busy folk don't have the time for. Occasionally I cooked for them too.'

So basically, she was a personal assistant stroke housekeeper but given a fancy job title. I try to arrange my face to suggest I'm impressed. 'I bet they're missing you,' I suggest. 'What are they going to do without you?'

She pulls a face. 'Honestly, I don't care. What about you? What's made your morning so rubbish?'

I sigh. 'I'm a self-employed bookkeeper, and I was pitching for a really big new client that would have turned my business around. I just discovered I didn't get the project.'

'Oh, I'm sorry. That must be gutting. But you know, I always say things happen for a reason, and there'll be a better opportunity around the corner.'

'You might be right.' I sigh. 'I'd have had to employ new staff, and that would be a nightmare in itself.' I'm surprised how empathetic Lauren is. For some stupid reason, I assumed she'd be an unpleasant person.

'I was thinking about training as an accountant at one point,' she says, taking a slow sip of her coffee.

'Why didn't you?'

'I had a stupid boyfriend at the time who said accountants were all boring. I can't believe I listened to him. Look at you – you're entrepreneurial, running your own business.'

'Funnily enough, I used to have a job a bit like yours. I was the personal assistant to a banker and ended up running much of his home and work life.'

'Really?'

'You know, it's never too late to retrain.' That's the first truly honest thing I've said to her.

'No, but I don't think I've got the brain capacity. I've got back in touch with all of the recruitment agencies, all except the one who placed me with the Deluccis. They're rubbish.'

'Who's that?'

'Saskia S Placements. They have a lot of actor-type clients on their books, and I'm through with that sort of person. I want to work for city people ideally.'

'Makes sense,' I say, committing the recruitment agency name to memory. 'Have they found someone new for the Deluccis?'

Lauren shrugs her shoulders. 'Honestly, don't know and don't care. Good luck to whoever they employ next.'

'Sounds like you're well out of it.'

'Yup. But money's tight now, so I really need to find something else. I'm sofa surfing at the moment, using my brother's address on my CV. As soon as I get a new job, I'll be able to rent a flat.'

I take another sip from my coffee and realise with surprise that it's empty. 'What are you doing to fill your days?' I ask.

'Going for runs in the park. I can't even go to the gym now because I lost the membership when I quit my job. It was one of the perks. It's about the only thing I miss.'

'You can always come as a guest to my gym,' I say before remembering that I'm not here to befriend Lauren.

'Seriously?' she asks, her eyes brightening. 'That's so kind of you.'

We swap phone numbers, for real this time. Much to my surprise, I realise that I like Lauren, that she could genuinely become a friend. It's just that I'm not sure how this new friendship will fit into my grand scheme, although a trip or two to the gym surely won't hurt.

'Right, I must be getting going,' I say, packing my things into my bag.

'It's so kind of you to get me the coffee, and despite the crap morning, it's been great to meet you. I'll take you up on the offer to go to your gym if that's okay?'

'I look forward to hearing from you,' I say as I stand up. And to my surprise, I really mean it.

ON MY WAY HOME, I do a Google search for Saskia S Placements. They call themselves an executive search agency for discerning private clients. I could send them a fake CV, but it's just so risky. The agency is bound to follow up on my references and discover they're fake, and that's even if they consider me for the job. There are bound to be numerous better candidates for the Deluccis, applicants who have been on Saskia S's books for years, people they know personally. It's a plum job, and I'm ninety-nine per cent sure I'd never get it if I apply in the traditional way. Besides, it'll be a waste of my time if they've already recruited someone new to the position. I reckon it calls for another few hours of snooping instead, just so I can check out their current situation. I take the bus back to Putney and slowly walk past the front of the Deluccis' grand white house. To the side of the entrance, there's a wall about three feet high, and as I peer over it, I see a little white dog, curled up asleep.

I hesitate. This dog must be Minnie, the one Lauren looked after.

'Minnie?' I say quietly. The dog opens one eye and looks up at me.

I have an idea. An idea that will make Goldie and her family pay. It's another crazy and impulsive idea, but it just might work.

I glance in both directions and open the gate, stepping inside the garden.

'Hey, Minnie,' I murmur, bending down and scooping her up into my arms. 'You want to come with me, little dog?'

8

GOLDIE

I'm glad Lauren is gone, but I'm struggling. Once again, everything is my responsibility. I have to do the cooking, organise the children's lives, manage the business, follow up new leads for funding for the next film and all the while try to keep my frequent migraines at bay. Easier said than done.

It's 5 pm, and both the kids and I are at home.

'Minnie, teatime!' I shout.

I wait to hear the clip-clop of the little dog's paws, or the scratching at the patio doors, but there's silence. I go outside into the garden.

'Minnie!' There's no answer. Where is she? I go back into the house and take the stairs two at a time, going first to Florian's room and then Rose's. Neither kid has seen Minnie for a while. Rose looks particularly concerned, which I'm slightly relieved about because at least it shows she has compassion for something other than herself. She's always viewed Minnie as her dog.

'Minnie!' I yell again, but there's silence. This is very unusual because Minnie rarely likes to be away from one of us for more than a few minutes at a time. She's a bichon frise, particularly friendly and universally loved. It's always been my fear that someone might leave the side gate open and Minnie could run into the road. She's not the brightest of little dogs, but we all love her nevertheless. A jolt of panic runs through me. I rush downstairs and out the front of the house, onto the road, scouring the street in both directions.

There's no sight of her. I then run back into the house.

'Rose, Florian, I need your help.'

Florian appears in his doorway. 'I can't find Minnie,' I explain. 'Can you help me look for her?'

Rose comes out onto the corridor, a look of concern on her face. She may loathe her parents, but she adores our dog. 'Has something happened to her, Mum?' she asks.

'I don't know. I let her out into the garden about an hour or so ago. Have either of you let her back in?'

They both shake their heads.

'Do you think she's got out of the garden?' Florian asks, wide-eyed.

'I hope not, but that's a possibility.' I don't mention the spate of dog thefts that has been reported in south London recently. As Minnie is an old dog, I rather hoped she'd be immune to such a horror. At least she's microchipped, and our phone number is on her collar. I try not to let my concern show on my face.

'Right, we're going to look for her. Florian, I want you to search the house. Check in every cupboard, under the beds, anywhere you can think of. Rose, you can turn left up Houndles Hill, and I'll go right. We all need to keep our mobiles on. We'll meet back here in thirty minutes if we haven't found her.' I try to quell my pounding heart. We all love Minnie so much, and I can't bear the thought of anything happening to her.

I hurry out of our drive, shouting Minnie's name and

hearing Rose do the same in the opposite direction. Then it crosses my mind to call the vet. If she's been hurt or if someone has found her, then they might have taken her there.

'Hello, it's Goldie Delucci calling. Has our dog, Minnie, been handed in, by any chance? We've lost her.'

'Oh goodness. No, I'm afraid we haven't had any dogs handed in today. You could try Battersea Dogs Home.'

I can't imagine why anyone would take her over there when both our telephone number and the vet's is on her name tag, but if we don't find her quickly, then I'll contact them.

Half an hour later, Minnie is nowhere to be seen. I really haven't got time for this, but Minnie has to take precedence over work. I hurry back home, meeting Rose in the driveway. Our normally tough-looking seventeen-year-old has tears in her eyes, and when I open my arms, she lets me hug her for the first time in years. 'Come on,' I say, my arm around her shoulders. 'Minnie will be fine. She's probably gone for a wander. Perhaps she's annoyed that she hasn't had a decent walk since Lauren left.'

'She could hardly jump over the wall by herself, could she?' Rose says, pulling away from me.

Florian appears in the doorway. 'Did you find her?'

We both shake our heads.

'I've got every confidence she'll be back soon. Let's have a drink, and then I'll take the car out and do a drive around.'

I'm pouring Florian a drink when the landline rings. I rush to get it.

It's a woman speaking. 'Hello. I've found a little white dog, and this is the telephone number on her collar.'

'Oh, you've got Minnie! That's wonderful!' I exclaim. 'We've been looking everywhere for her. Where did you find her?' I smile at the kids and give them a thumbs up. I've never seen Rose look so relieved.

'She was trotting along all by herself at the top of Houndles Hill. She seems perfectly okay. I'll bring her back to you if you give me your address.'

'Thank you so much. That's incredibly kind.' I give her our address.

'Great. I'll be with you in about ten minutes.'

A FEW MINUTES LATER, the doorbell rings, and I hurry to open the door. The woman standing on the doorstep has a leather laptop bag slung over one shoulder and is holding Minnie in her arms. Mid-thirties, at a guess, her auburn hair is neatly cropped, and she has smiling dark eyes. She's wearing smart navy blue trousers and a beige raincoat and looks as if she's just come from an office meeting.

'I cannot thank you enough,' I say as she hands Minnie to me. 'We've been looking everywhere for you, you little monster.' I kiss the top of Minnie's head before handing her to Rose, who is standing right behind me.

'Please, you must come in for a coffee if you have time. It's so good of you to bring her back.'

The woman glances at her watch.

'Only if you have time,' I repeat, rather hoping that she says no. 'You've been so kind.'

'I do have time, actually. That's very kind of you.' She holds out her hand. 'I'm Simone Carver.'

'It's lovely to meet you, Simone. I'm Goldie Delucci, and Rose and Florian, who have now vanished, are my two kids. Come in.' I know you shouldn't judge someone on looks, but she's wearing smart clothes, and frankly, anyone who rescues Minnie is deserving of a coffee at the very least.

Simone's eyes widen. 'It's a beautiful home you have here.'

'Thank you. We love it.' She follows me into the kitchen.

'Would you like a coffee, tea or something stronger?'

She laughs. It's a gentle laugh, with a ring to it. 'A little early for something stronger. I've been in meetings all day and have drunk way too much coffee. A tea would be lovely. Thank you.'

'What do you do if you've been in meetings all day?'

Simone looks a little bashful. 'Not exactly meetings, more like interviews. I'm looking for a new job.'

'What is it that you do?'

'I've been living in Singapore for the past three years, working as a personal assistant to a family. Both parents worked in investment banking. They're relocating to Australia, and although they begged me to go with them, it's just too far away. I decided to come home.'

'Really?' My hand hovers over the teapot. I don't say anything, not yet, because I'm not impulsive, but what an extraordinary coincidence this is. I'm still waiting for Saskia S's shortlist of candidates to interview for Lauren's position, and frankly, I'm getting impatient. I need the post filling yesterday. 'How do you take your tea?'

'Just a splash of milk, no sugar, please. This is so kind of you.'

'Oh goodness, it's me who is thankful to you. Minnie isn't very streetwise despite being a London born and bred dog. It's always been my terror that she'd escape and get run over.'

'Has she escaped before?'

'No.' I shake my head. 'That's what's weird. The gate was closed, and I've no idea how she got out. I'll have to ask the gardener to double-check all the fencing.' I carry the teapot and cups over to the table, along with the carton of milk. 'So are you a dog lover?'

'Absolutely. I'm determined that the next family I work for has a dog. I love them and really missed not having a dog around in Singapore. How long have you been living here?'

'Gosh, nearly a decade now. We gutted the house. It was quite the project.'

'It's beautiful. I love this table.' She runs her palm over the smooth surface. 'Are you an interior designer?'

I snort, which probably isn't the most appropriate response, and she glances up with surprise. 'No. I hired someone to make this place look lovely. My husband and I run a film production company. We're in post-production for our second film and are raising funds and casting for the next one. Life is crazily hectic.'

'And no doubt you could have done without losing little Minnie this afternoon.'

'Quite.' I laugh. 'So tell me more about the responsibilities in your previous job.'

'Lots of admin, being super-organised, being a bit of a general dogsbody, taking the children to school and occasionally cooking meals, although they did have a cook and a maid. I'm also a qualified bookkeeper, so I managed their household accounts.'

I stare at Simone, and she tilts her head to one side, smiling at me. 'Is everything alright?' she asks.

'This is probably going to sound very weird, but we recently parted company with our concierge, a woman who held the same sort of role that you had, and actually I'm about to start interviewing applicants for the position. I don't suppose you'd be interested, would you?'

Simone places her cup on the table, and her face brightens into a wide smile. 'You're joking?'

I shake my head. 'Is it too much of a coincidence?'

'It's extraordinary. Is the vacancy with an agency?'

'Yes. Saskia S Placements. Have you come across them?'

Simone shakes her head. 'Can't say I have.'

'If you're interested in applying, we wouldn't have to go through them.'

'That would be just silly, paying commission unnecessarily,' she says, and then she flushes with embarrassment. 'Assuming you think I'm the right person for the job, of course. I only rescued Minnie. I may not be right at all.'

'It's a live-in position ideally. We have a self-contained flat in the basement. Perks include gym membership, the use of a car and private health insurance.' I tell her the salary, and her eyes widen. My dad used to say, pay peanuts you get monkeys, and despite the unsavoury expression, I agree with him. Not that it worked out well with Lauren.

'I'd love to interview for the position, Goldie. It's almost too good to be true. Not that I know anything about film production companies though.'

'No need to. We try to keep home and work life separate.' We didn't always achieve that with Lauren, but I want the next person in the job to concentrate on managing our home. 'Why don't you come back tomorrow, and we'll do a proper interview. Bring your CV, and we'll take it from there.'

'Wow! Thank you so much.' Simone stands up, and we shake hands.

THE NEXT MORNING doesn't get off to a great start because there's another article in the *Daily Mail* about the tragic death of actress Alison Greystone. The media are speculating whether our film, *The Insomniac*, will be a worthy memorial for her. I mean, it's ridiculous. It annoys me, but at the same time I suppose it's good for business. It puts our name out there, gets the public interested in the upcoming film. Yet I also feel sad for poor Ally. I try not to think about what happened to her, what happened to my car, because it's just so gruesome, and with everything that's going on, I have to maintain my own sanity. But I can't bury my head in the sand when it comes to publicity for *The Insomniac*, so I go online and look on Twitter, the thermometer of our industry.

Damn. Someone has posted that the inquest showed there were drugs in Ally's bloodstream, and they're speculating whether other members of the cast were using too. That I can do without. As I'm watching, the likes and the retweeting go up and up. How the hell do I stop this? I can't let the rumour mill get in the way of our success. The financial pressures are horrendous. *The Insomniac* must do well in the box offices, not just to give a good return to our investors (and Braun's parents and us) but also so we get real traction and Delucci Productions is taken seriously. Our first film, *The Alsatian Files*, did alright, but it wasn't a runaway success. *The Insomniac* has to be. My head pounds, and I swallow some painkillers as a preemptive strike. A migraine is another thing I need to nip in the bud.

On the dot of 9 am, I call Liberator PR.

'Can I speak to Lucille Kane, please.'

'Goldie!' Lucille exclaims as she comes on the line. She has a deep, bellowing voice. 'How can I help?'

I used Lucille's PR agency when we started Delucci Productions, and she's done a good job for us, helping raise our profile, but I haven't needed to use her for crisis management. That might be about to change. I explain about Ally's death and the current media speculation.

'We can sort that,' Lucille says. 'Reputation management is so important these days, but you need to be sure that there's no truth in the rumours; otherwise the press will have a field day.'

I hesitate. 'Look, drugs were found in Ally's system, but it doesn't mean they were widespread on set. It was a one-off, tragic situation.'

'Fair enough,' she says. 'Leave this with me.'

After we've finished the conversation, I wonder. I can't know for sure whether any of the other members of our cast and crew had or have drugs problems. Life on set is Braun's responsibility, but perhaps I need to investigate. It takes so long to build up a business, to get a good reputation, but both can be slayed in an instant. That's not a risk I can take.

I'M STARTLED by Florian walking into the room. 'Mum, that woman who found Minnie is at the door.'

I glance at my watch. I've let the morning slip away, and I'm not in the slightest bit prepared for the interview with Simone. Not that it should be a problem. I've interviewed hundreds of people over the years and sat in on numerous auditions. I'm good at reading people and can see through nerves to true potential.

I hurry through to the hallway to greet her. 'Simone,' I say, my hand extended. 'Good to see you again.'

'How's Minnie today?' she asks. On cue the dog scampers towards us. Simone bends down and rubs her head.

'How's my little friend?'

'Would you like a tea or coffee?' I ask.

'No, I'm fine, thanks.'

I guide Simone into my office. I have the larger of the two studies downstairs because I spend the most time working from home. It's a bright room that looks out towards our well-manicured garden and the magnolia tree, which is magnificent in early spring. I've decorated it in a New England style with white furniture and a large sheepskin rug on the floor.

'Have a seat.'

Simone hands me her CV, and I glance through it. It's impressive, although most of her work has been for overseas families.

'I see that you trained as a bookkeeper, but how come you changed track?'

'A friend of the family was looking for a personal assistant, but someone who was good with numbers, and I just fell into the job. In many ways, I find it more interesting. I'm able to use my financial training but also do much more varied work. I'm the sort of person who likes to get their hands dirty. I'll even do the cleaning if it needs to be done.'

This woman sounds like a dream.

'Have you got any experience of being around sulky teenagers?'

Simone laughs. 'Our parents died young, and I pretty much brought up my younger sibling. Teenagers don't worry me.'

'I'm sorry to hear that.'

She shrugs. 'It was a long time ago.'

'How would your last employers describe you?'

'Good question,' she says, glancing upwards and to the left. 'Conscientious, an eye for detail, a bit stubborn, but hopefully in a good way and totally loyal. I think one of the most important things when working in someone's home is to understand how vital confidentiality is and to be discreet and utterly trustworthy.'

I nod because she's spot on there. It reminds me that I've been tracking what film critics and the general public are saying about our films, but I haven't kept an eye on Lauren's online presence. She signed a confidentiality agreement of course, but a dishonest person like her might be persuaded to divulge personal information on us as a family. Perhaps I should mention it to Lucille.

'Have you got any questions for me?' I ask.

'Just what are the key responsibilities in the role?'

I talk her through all the admin tasks that Lauren used to do, overseeing the kids when I'm not at home, managing both

Braun's and my diaries, booking any foreign trips, paying all the bills. I explain that we have a cleaner who comes in twice a week, and I cook when I have time, but realistically we get meals in.

'I love cooking,' Simone says. 'And I'd be happy to help out from time to time.'

'Would you like to see the flat?' I ask, standing up. This woman is absolutely perfect. She's a few years older than Lauren, which must be helpful, and she has an air of confidence and efficiency about her. I hope Braun will like her as much as I do.

Half an hour later, which speeds past and I only notice because I've set an alarm on my phone, I offer Simone the job. She looks utterly delighted.

'How soon can you start?'

'On Monday?' she says hesitantly. 'I can move in over the weekend.'

I clap my hands. 'That's wonderful!'

It isn't until the middle of the night that I realise I really should have checked her references before offering her the job. I'll just add that to my to-do list over the weekend. My gut feeling tells me that Simone will be ideal for the job.

9

SIMONE

Considering this is a position that I didn't really want or need, I seem to be settling in rather well. The flat is small in comparison to mine, but then I only brought a couple of suitcases with me. I don't intend to stay for more than a month, and I can always nip home if I need something. The first evening, Goldie invites me to join the family for supper. They are already sitting at the kitchen table when I arrive, and I feel awkward.

'Braun, meet Simone.'

He runs his eyes over me slowly, as if he is assessing me, less for my suitability for the role as their family concierge or whatever ridiculous title they've given me, but more as if he's appraising my physical attributes. Or maybe I am being too sensitive. Perhaps that's just how he's used to evaluating actors for his films.

'So you're Minnie's rescuer,' he says, holding out his hand so that I have to walk over to him to shake it. 'Welcome to the family.' He squeezes my fingers painfully hard.

Braun is swarthy looking, with oiled-back dark hair and a

short-cut beard. He's well built, with the swagger of someone
who thinks he's good looking. Okay, maybe I'm being unfair
on him because I decided I didn't like the guy before I even
met him, but he is supremely confident and expects his
family to defer to his opinion. I don't find him in the slightest
bit attractive, but I can see how some women might. Confidence is a great libido enhancer.

Rose totally ignores both of her parents and eye-rolls
whenever they talk to her, whereas Florian really doesn't say
very much at all.

'Do you eat meat?' Goldie asks. 'I totally forgot to ask
whether you have any dietary requirements.'

'No, none,' I say.

'In which case you're the only member of this household
who doesn't. Braun won't eat fish, I can't eat anything like
chocolate or cheese as they trigger my migraines, Florian is
allergic to dairy, and Rose is vegan. Last month she was
vegetarian.'

'Just because I'm the only person who's making a stand
for what is and isn't right doesn't mean you can mock me!'
Rose glowers at her mother.

'Keep your knickers on,' Braun says.

I can almost see the steam rising from Rose's head.
Florian avoids any conflict by scratching his napkin and
chewing his nails. Interesting family dynamics.

'Would you prefer roast lamb or the bean stew, or a bit of
both?' Goldie asks.

'The lamb would be lovely, thank you.'

OVER THE NEXT couple of days, I keep my head down and get
used to the job. And yes, I've been settling in well. It's Goldie
who surprises me. She's a much nicer person than I had

anticipated her being. As the producer of a successful film company, I rather assumed she'd be brash and no-nonsense, demanding with pretensions of superiority. Instead, I reckon she's an overworked, frazzled mother with a demanding job who is barely keeping things together. She is permanently harried, juggling incessant phone calls, yet still making the effort to smile at me and be patient when I can't find things. She is less tolerant with her kids, particularly Rose, but then Rose is only communicative when she wants something. I've also noticed that Goldie takes medication, lots of ibuprofen, paracetamol and a prescribed drug called rizatriptan. I've looked it up – it's for migraines, and from the way Goldie holds her head and flinches when she thinks no one is watching, I reckon she's in pain a lot of the time. I can't decide if it's annoying or just as well, but Braun is rarely at home, and I've had little interaction with him. He's definitely more of an enigma, and I will need to go out of my way to understand him better. But even he has been nothing but charming towards me.

One of my many admin jobs is to make sure the Deluccis' household bills get paid on time. They've given me a laptop, and I have to maintain a spreadsheet, double-check their direct debits and put any day-to-day invoices in a file, listing the dates they need to be paid. This folder has to go onto Goldie's desk, and each Friday afternoon, she pays any outstanding bills. Once they're paid, it's my job to file them. I also have access to her personal emails. I organise the online shopping and bring anything to her attention that I think needs addressing. This morning, Goldie receives an email from the garage requesting feedback on her new car. This could be just the opportunity I'm looking for.

Goldie strides into the kitchen, holding an empty mug.

'Would you like me to make you a cuppa?' I ask.

'Thanks, Simone.'

'Am I right in thinking you recently got a new car? It's just you've received an email from the garage.'

She runs her fingers through her hair, and I notice that her roots need touching up. 'Oh yes. It's fully electric, so it'd be good if you could double-check that it's properly charged each morning. I could check on my phone, but frankly, I rarely remember. It would just about crease me if I had to drive to the studios or on location and discover I've run out of charge.'

'Sure, no problem,' I reassure her. 'What happened to your old car? Was it just time for an upgrade?' I have my back to Goldie as I'm pouring milk into her mug. Just as well, as I wouldn't want her to see my face.

'My old one was totalled by some girl at work. A nightmare and a terrible accident. Honestly, I try not to think about it too much. The repercussions are massive and relentless.'

Too bloody right they are. I spill a bit of milk and hurriedly wipe it up with a dishcloth.

'Here you go,' I say, handing her the mug, but I have to pass it over with both hands because I'm shaking. Fortunately, Goldie doesn't seem to notice.

'The car file is in the filing cabinet if you need it. Just answer the email and say everything's fine with the new car. Thanks, Simone.'

And she leaves the kitchen.

It gives me the opportunity to rifle through the files. Goldie and Braun keep their household paperwork in a filing cabinet in their large living room. The bespoke painted oak cabinetry includes bookshelves either side of the fireplace and a bar with drinks cabinets on the side wall opposite the door. In contrast to the austere kitchen, this room is comfortable, with large cream sofas and a huge standard lamp made from feathers. The walls are covered with modern art, mostly vibrant paintings of people and a nude torso, which I'm guessing might be Goldie.

Bizarrely, the filing cabinet is next to a wine fridge. Perhaps it's the only place they could fit a hanging file cabinet, or perhaps they reckoned they would need a strong drink every time they went through their personal affairs. Either way, it means that I can have a good look without being disturbed, as none of the family tend to come in here until the evenings. Lauren seems to have done a good job because everything is neatly labelled, and within each folder, items are listed chronologically. I pull out the file that says Goldie's Car. I discard the first few documents, which relate to the new car, and then see the correspondence from the insurers about the car in which my sister was killed. If I was hoping for anything that might throw further light on the circumstances of the accident, I'm disappointed. There is a letter from the claims assessor confirming that the car was a write-off. Another one saying that pending the police investigation and the inquest, Goldie will receive full payment for the value of the car. There's nothing to suggest the insurance company's investigation was any different to that of the police. Although the car was insured for anyone to drive, because Ally took it without Braun's or Goldie's permission, it was considered stolen. Neither of the Deluccis were held accountable. I take the opportunity to flick through some more of their paperwork, but I find nothing of interest. And now, at the end of this first week, I wonder whether I'm going to find anything of relevance. Perhaps it's better if I take a two-pronged approach. I will contact Kit and meet up with some other friends of Ally's to find out what was really causing my sister so much stress before she died, as well as continue probing into the Deluccis' affairs.

. . .

I CALL Leila and get Kit's phone number. If he thinks it's strange that I'm calling him, he doesn't say anything.

'It was great to meet you the other night,' I say.

'You too. I can't stop thinking about Ally,' Kit says.

'She was so stressed in those last few weeks. What was it really like on set?'

'Honestly, Simone, it was just the same as on any other film set except the hours were even longer. The difference is, Ally wasn't used to it. Most of us don't have families either, so she was having to juggle a lot.'

'What are the Deluccis really like?'

'Braun's a prat. By the way he prances around, it's like he thinks he's the next Kubrick or Scorsese. I mean, he's good enough, but I think it's Goldie who's the real talent behind the productions. Anyway, lacklustre directing can often be redeemed by great editing, and Martin, the editor, has got some excellent credits to his name. We'll see when the film's finished. I hope it's good because I need more work after the play in Chichester, and it will be Ally's – well, you know.'

I suppose he means it's her swan song. The only chance she'll ever get at critical acclaim. I swallow hard. I know I already asked him the question, but I ask again, hoping that he doesn't remember too much detail about our conversation in the pub.

'That night she died, were the Deluccis on set?'

'I don't know. I wasn't there.' That's what Kit told me when we last spoke, but I wanted to be sure. 'It was only the cast and crew involved in the final scene, and then, according to my mates, when it wrapped, they got the beers out and drank. Goldie probably wasn't there. As the producer, she was mainly behind the scenes, but I expect Braun was. He spent a lot of time with Martin, the editor, but I can't tell you anything about that evening. I'm sorry.'

We're both silent for a long moment.

'Look, I've got an idea,' Kit says. 'I'm going to a party on Saturday night. It's the unofficial wrap party organised by Tristan, the lead actor, and everyone will be there except the Deluccis. It should have been held the week we finished up, but what with Ally's death, it just didn't seem right. If you want to know what happened to Ally that night, why don't you come along? You can be my plus one.'

'Really? The thing is, Kit, I can't have anyone knowing who I really am. I mean, it would look like I'm spying, attending the party because I'm Ally's sister, and that's just weird.'

'I'm an actor, Simone. I can say you're a wannabe actress or my latest girlfriend or my mother's maiden aunt. Whoever you want to be.'

I laugh. 'Firstly, you're gay, and secondly, do I really look old enough to be the maiden aunt?'

'So you'll join me?'

'Yes. Where and when?'

As soon as I walk into the house, I realise I really do look like Kit's dull aunt. Not due to my age, because the people here are anywhere between eighteen and sixty, but because I'm wearing black trousers and a pale pink silk blouse. Everyone else here has a style, whether it's crazily coloured, diaphanous kaftans or all black with strategic tears and safety pins. I'm just ordinary, boring probably. Whether that will help me stay unnoticed or make me stand out as the misfit, I'm not sure. I certainly feel that way. The thumping music is loud, coloured lights flash in time to the beat, and everyone is talking – or rather shouting – so that the assault on my ears is almost too much. I've noticed that few of my friends smoke anymore, but not so here. People are standing at open windows and in doorways, puffing on cigarettes, and the smell of nicotine mingles with weed and strangely scented candles. I'm surprised. I thought actors would need to take care of their voices and their health.

'Don't look so horrified,' Kit says, taking my elbow and steering me through the packed living room into the kitchen. 'You're just like your sister, aren't you?'

This is a big house, not the size of the Deluccis', but clearly the owner is someone with eclectic taste and money. And someone who loves colour. Every room is a riot of mismatched reds, oranges and purples, the rooms plastered with pictures and posters, and many photos of Tristan promoting his films.

'Who's who?' I ask Kit as he hands me a glass of white wine.

'The loudest people are the actors, the more normal' – he says the word using his fingers to delineate quotes – 'are the crew. That's Tristan over there.' He points to a man with a chiselled jaw and dark blue eyes, his white shirt open down to his navel, revealing a hairless chest and six-pack, although bearing in mind his face is plastered all over the walls of this house, I could have worked that one out.

'Who can you introduce me to? Who was there on Ally's last night?'

Kit raises an eyebrow and glances around the room. 'Martin. He's the editor and spends most of the time with Braun, particularly these days. He's the old geezer over there. Follow me.'

I hesitate for a moment because what if Martin ever comes to the Deluccis' house and recognises me? But then I discount my concern. I'll worry about that at a later date if I have to. We take a circuitous route towards Martin, as Kit is stopped by friends and colleagues, and I hang back, trying to be as unnoticeable as possible. Not difficult. As it turns out, Martin starts walking towards us, so Kit stops him.

'My friend here has a younger sibling who's interested in getting into film editing. Any chance she could pick your brains for a minute?'

Martin must be late fifties or early sixties, with a worn, leathery face. He is bald on the top of his head, but the hair around the sides is long, almost to his shoulders. Wearing a black long-sleeved T-shirt, he gives off the air of being an old rocker. He looks as unimpressed by the idea of me asking him about editing as I am. What the hell am I meant to say to Martin?

'I've got to be honest, I don't know the first thing about what you do!' I say, grimacing awkwardly. 'But I promised my sister I'd ask. My name is Nina, by the way.' I've no idea why that name slipped into my head and just hope I remember it. Annoyingly, Kit has instantly disappeared, so he won't know that I've just renamed myself. I curse myself for my stupidity. There was no reason not to use my real name.

Martin sighs unsubtly, and I get the sense he's looking over my shoulder, trying to be rescued by someone more interesting than me. 'I assemble the footage, a bit like putting a jigsaw together to refine the overall story. I work really closely with the director.'

'Braun Delucci?'

'That's the one,' he says with a deadpan face.

'I gather he's a very talented director,' I say, twirling my wine glass between my fingers.

'Yup,' Martin says unconvincingly.

'Kit was saying that you're up against really tight deadlines on this film. Is that normal?'

'Yes, this is no different to any film. A conflict between creative vision and deadlines and budgets.'

'It must be interesting having Braun as the director and Goldie as the producer.'

He runs his tongue over his front teeth and then takes a swig from the bottle he's holding. I realise with surprise that it's orange juice not beer.

'So what do you do, Nina?'

I hesitate for a moment, because I'd already forgotten my name was supposed to be Nina. 'Boring. I'm a bookkeeper. You can see why my sister doesn't want to follow in my footsteps.'

'Money makes the world go around.'

'I guess it must be interesting dynamics in the Delucci household with Goldie holding the film company's purse strings.'

'I don't get involved in stuff like that.'

Oh, this is difficult. Martin is introverted and really tricky to talk to. 'So Braun doesn't talk to you about anything except the creative side of the film?'

'Of course not.'

And then I decide I might as well straight up ask the question I want the answer to.

'I heard about the tragic death of one of your actresses.' I swallow hard. 'I gather you were with Braun that night when it happened.'

He stares at me then, his eyes narrowed, shifting his weight from foot to foot, and then he glances away, as if his eyes are repelled from looking at me.

'Why are you asking me a question like that?' he says eventually, his body edging away from me, but he's standing right next to a kitchen unit, so there's nowhere for him to go.

'I was just curious.' My heart is thumping now, and I wish Kit were here, but I can't see him anywhere.

And then it's as if a switch flips inside him, and he turns

from defensive to aggressive. 'What's it got to do with you anyway? Who are you? A journalist or something?'

'No, absolutely not.'

'Well, we don't like people sticking their noses into things. We're a family here and a grieving family at that. It's shit what happened, and I have to sit there and watch her on screen every day, knowing she's dead.'

'I'm sorry, you're right. I think I'd better get another drink.' I hold up my now empty wine glass and take the opportunity to weave between the drinkers and slip out of the kitchen. When I'm in the hallway, I have to squeeze between people, apologising for stepping on feet, not that I think anyone is sober enough to notice or care. Once I'm at the front door, I quickly glance backwards to make sure that Martin hasn't followed me, although I can't imagine that he would. I don't see him, but I also can't see Kit. I hesitate for a moment because it's rude leaving without saying goodbye to Kit, but I don't want to go looking for him. Instead I send him a quick text; then I slip out of the front door, closing it behind me. And then I run. I'm not sure why, but I feel so uncomfortable being here. Martin's reaction was weird, but then my questions probably were too. He was definitely shifty, keeping something from me, yet what, I'm very far from knowing. When I reach the tube station and jump straight onto a train, the musty smell and squeaking of the brakes are strangely reassuring. I'm happy to be on my way back to Putney.

A FEW DAYS LATER, I don't feel like I'm any further forwards in discovering anything about the Deluccis or the night Ally died, yet I'm not ready to give up. I took Florian from school to a friend's house this afternoon and was surprised to find Rose already home when I returned. Quite often she isn't back until supper time. I'm upstairs putting away Goldie's dry cleaning when I hear keys in the front door and Braun's voice. It's unusual for him to be home this early in the afternoon. I glance out of the window and to my dismay see that Martin is stepping into the house. I can't possibly let him see me. I knew I should have been more careful.

'Simone, are you there?' Braun shouts up the stairs.

I freeze. What if Martin is standing in the hall next to Braun and spots me? I step backwards into the corridor, to keep myself out of view.

'How can I help, Braun?'

'Can you bring us a couple of black coffees into my study?'

'Sure,' I say. But how am I going to do that without being seen!

With Goldie out at a meeting, the only other person in the house is Rose. I'm going to have to get Rose to help out because there's no way I can let Martin see me. I knock on Rose's door. There's no answer, so I gently open it and poke my head around. She's seated in front of her laptop at her desk, headphones over her ears.

'Rose?'

She spins around, jamming the lid of her laptop down.

'What is it?'

'Would you mind making two cups of black coffee for your dad and his guest.'

'Eh, yeah. I would mind. That's your job, isn't it?'

'I've got to do something urgent for your mum. She just called me.'

'And Dad can't wait?'

'No, Rose,' I say, raising my voice a fraction. She really is a nightmare girl. 'I'm asking you to go and do it now and without making a fuss, please. You do know how to make coffee, I assume?'

She glowers at me, and for a moment I wonder if we're

going to be at an impasse, but then she pulls the headphones off, throws them onto the desk and gets up from her chair. She pushes past me but not before I hear her mutter 'bitch' under her breath.

Have I got away with it?

10

ROSE

Nothing ever changes in this house. How dare Simone treat me as if I'm a member of staff! And why the hell can't Dad get his own damned coffee? He's quite able to make it in the mornings for his breakfast, so why not now? Is it because he's trying to show off to some colleague that making coffee is beneath him?

As I storm past Simone, who disappears back into Mum and Dad's bedroom, I'm inclined to walk straight out of the door and to hell with them all.

Thank goodness for school. Wow, I can't believe I'm thinking that, but often the school holidays and half terms are worse than term time. At least when I'm meant to be at school during the day, I'm officially out of this house. Of course, I don't actually hang at school. It's so boring, and as long as I sign in first thing, I really don't think anyone notices I'm gone. Today, I'm researching a new scam and waiting for my Amazon delivery. So I do as Simone asks and make the coffee, although I spit into both cups because, well, why wouldn't I? It makes me feel better.

I carry them into Dad's study. He's sitting there crouched

over his desk with some old geezer sitting next to him. I plonk the cups down on his desk.

'Where's Simone?' Dad asks.

'Doing something for Mum. I'm your skivvy for the afternoon, although don't get your hopes up because I'm going out shortly.'

Dad grins at me. 'This is Rose, my gobby daughter.'

The man just nods at me. He looks like a miserable sod.

Fortunately my Amazon delivery arrives about ten minutes later. Tomorrow is going to be the big day.

I SHOVE the black suit I nicked a couple of weeks ago into my rucksack and take it to school. After the first lesson – English, where I totally zone out because who gives a toss if Hamlet's mum is shagging his uncle, I nip to the bathroom, and when the bell has rung and everyone is back in class, I change into it. I look ridiculous, like an undertaker or something, but hopefully it'll do. Shrugging my khaki parka over the top, I slip out of school, through the fire exit that the catering staff use to have a smoke. I look like one of them dressed up like this – minus the pink apron, of course.

This is going to be a fun one. It might be hard to pull off because I'm female and young, but it's got to be worth a try.

When I'm on the bus, I pin the badge I got off Amazon onto the lapel of the suit jacket. It's gold and shiny and says Hotel Porter. I swallow my snigger.

Today, I head for Paddington. There are lots of hotels over there, and all I need to do is find one that isn't upmarket enough to have its own porter, which shouldn't be hard, as quite a few of them are dives. I walk up and down a couple of streets, and when I've found a hotel that looks middling smart, I slip around the street corner, take off my parka and stuff it into my rucksack. I leave the rucksack in someone's basement area, underneath a small metal table.

The hotel is mid-terrace, a white stucco building with wide marble steps that go up to the front door. There are a couple of topiary olive trees either side of the door, which is kept propped open. I've seen guests come out. All I need to do is wait for some to arrive.

This is the part of any scam that gets me the most pumped up. Adrenaline is racing through my veins, and I jig my right foot up and down before catching myself and remembering that I need to look blasé, as if I belong here. And then I see a black cab indicating to the left, slowing down as it pulls up in front of the hotel. I could whoop with delight as I watch the couple get out. They look well dressed. She's wearing high heels and one of those raincoats with a plaid pattern, an ugly thing but I'm pretty sure it's designer, and she's wearing a lot of gold around her neck, big dangling earrings and lots of multicoloured rings. He's a good-looking black man, in a suit, pulling out notes to give to the cabbie. I didn't think anyone carried cash around these days. And then to my further delight, the man tugs out a medium-sized suitcase.

'Good afternoon, sir,' I say as I step forwards. 'Welcome to the Barringstyle Hotel. May I help you with your luggage?'

He gives me a strange look, and for a moment I wonder if he thinks I'm too puny looking or if he doesn't speak English. I'm ready to say I'm stronger than I look, but I don't need to, because the woman turns to him and says, 'Come on, darling.'

'If you'd like to check in at reception, I will make sure that your suitcase is brought up to your room.' I smile sweetly at him, fingering the hotel porter badge with my left hand because I know that even if it's just at a subconscious level, his eyes will be drawn to it.

'Thank you,' he says and hands me the suitcase. I watch as he strides up the steps after his wife and disappears into the darkness of the lobby.

A second later, the taxi has gone. And a second after that, I'm legging it. But the suitcase is heavier than it looks, and by the time I'm around the corner, I'm panting. I slip behind a tree on the pavement and unpin the badge.

It isn't until I'm taking off the black jacket that I notice a guy leaning against a fast-looking motorbike. He's staring at me, an amused expression on his face. I stare back at him. He's attractive, with thick, messy brown hair, the hint of a beard and a square jaw. He's got a small scar on his cheek and another one that cuts through his left eyebrow.

'What are you looking at?' I sneer at him.

He runs his hand over his fast-looking, shiny red motor-bike and then steps forwards towards me.

'I'm Tony,' he says.

'Yeah, well, I'm Madonna, and I couldn't give a shit.'

'Nope, you're not. But I know what you did, and you're good at it.'

I freeze. Did he see me? Does he know that the suitcase I'm still holding the handle of isn't mine? Oh God!

'Are you a policeman?' I whisper. 'Undercover?'

He laughs then. A full belly laugh as if it's the funniest thing he's ever heard.

'Do I look like a copper?'

'No,' I say, because now I'm really not sure. He could be a special agent or something. I wonder if I should run again. I can always leave the case behind, and he can have it if he wants.

'I'm not the police, about as far from being the police as is possible.' He talks with an East End accent. 'But you're good at what you do, and I was wondering if you'd like to work with me?'

'Doing what?'

He leans back against his bike and crosses his arms, his biceps bulging. 'That little scam you pulled off there, nicking the case. What are you going to do with it now? And it's not like you can pull off another stunt because how are you going to manage two cases or a whole pile of them? Got a car, have you?'

I shake my head.

'We can use my bike as the getaway vehicle when we're working together, and I've got ways to dispose of the stuff you nick, so you'll get cash in return. I'm like you. A loner and good at what I do, but sometimes two heads are better than one. What do you reckon?'

I pause for a long moment because this has totally caught me off guard.

'How do I know this isn't some sort of trap?'

He opens up his arms. 'You don't. But it isn't. I just thought that you and me could be good together, but if you don't agree, then no harm done, and I'll just be on my way.'

I hesitate. He's really good looking, and isn't this exactly what I wished for? To have a partner in crime. 'How do I know you won't screw me over?'

'How do I know you won't do the same?' He has a cheeky grin, and the way he looks at me makes my stomach flip. I'm not sure anyone has looked at me like that before. Not in the desperate way some of the boys at school do, but in a controlled and sexy way, as if he's hungry for me.

'Look, I've never done something like this before, either,' he says, stepping away from his bike, and holding out the palms of his hands. 'I mean, I get it's a bit creepy me coming onto you like this, a stranger and all. But what you and me do, it's lonely work, isn't it? And I think we can achieve more with you being a woman and me a man.'

If anyone else had called me a woman, I might be riled by

it, because gender stereotypes are so demeaning, but the way Tony says it makes me feel good. Really good, because he sees me as being a person in my own right, an adult and not just some teenage girl. I'm going to give him a chance. What have I got to lose?

'I've been a fence for other people,' he says quietly, stepping towards me and putting his hand on my arm. It sends tingles all the way through me. 'I've got contacts, but I understand if you prefer to do things by yourself.'

'No. It'd be good to work together. You're right, there's only so much I can do working alone. I'm up for it.'

He claps his hands together, and that sexy smile splits his face. 'Hey, partner!' he says, and we bump knuckles. 'What do you fancy doing next, then?'

'Um, I need to get rid of this suitcase and just collect my rucksack.' I point awkwardly to the basement where I dumped my things.

'Sure. What's your name, pretty lady?'

'It's Rose,' I say, trying not to blush.

'Sweet-smelling rose. Why's that no surprise? Come along then, Rose. You and me have got work to do. First we need to get that case opened and take out anything that's of value. Don't worry, this one's all yours.'

Tony takes the case from me and lifts it as if it's as light as a pillow. I follow him as we stride quickly along the street and then slip into an alleyway between two houses. He does it so quickly, forcing the case open, rifling through everything and selecting designer clothes, some jewellery and an iPad, shoving them into his rucksack and mine. He then zips the case up and leaves it standing there in the alley.

'Right, we need to get moving.'

As we get to his bike, he hands me a helmet, a second one that I hadn't noticed was there. 'Slip this on, lovely Rose.' And then he swings his leg over the bike seat, and I realise that I'm meant to do the same, sitting behind him. This is so dope. I've never been on a motorbike before, and this one's a real beast. I mean it's huge, and when Tony starts it up, it literally roars.

'Hold on tight,' he says, and I clasp my arms around him, feeling the tautness of his body. I've been with boys, but Tony's a man, and he feels so different. And then we're off.

It's so exciting, the wind tearing past us, weaving in and out of cars and red London buses, swerving down side streets, and then he's pulling up somewhere behind Leicester Square.

'What are your best scams, partner?' he asks, casually pulling his helmet off. I'm still trying to catch my breath after the ride.

'Nicking credit cards, pretending to be a waiter. Shoplifting. Pickpocketing. But that gets a bit boring.'

'Show me how you do the waitress gig.'

'Okay,' I say. I haven't got my apron with me today, but I'm still wearing the smart black trousers, so it'll have to do. And I do well. An hour later, I've got two American Express cards, a Visa card, and then I nick some designer jewellery.

'You rock it!' Tony says. 'I'll take the jewellery and the cards off you and how about...' He takes out a massive wad of cash from his jeans pocket. I mean, how did he even fit all of that in there? And then starts counting out fifty-quid notes. 'Reckon five hundred quid is about right for the afternoon's work, what do you say?' He hands me ten notes.

'You serious?' I ask. I've never had that much money. It's totally crazy.

'You're worth it, partner. Right. I've got to get moving. Why don't I take you home?'

'I live south of the river.'

'Well, that's a coincidence. Me too. Where shall I take you?'

'Putney. Is that too far?'

'For you, beautiful Rose, nowhere is too far. There'll be traffic this time of day. Shall we get going?'

I can't wipe the smile off my face as we sweep through London's streets, slower now because it's rush hour, and even though Tony weaves through the traffic jams, it still takes a long time. But I don't care. I'm on top of the world. I've got serious cash in my bag, and my arms are around this gorgeous man, my partner. If only I could tell the kids at school, they'd be so green. Perhaps I'll tell Charlie, but then I decide I won't. Tony's going to be my delicious secret.

As we're waiting at the lights the far side of Putney Bridge, he turns to me. 'What's the address, then?'

I decide not to tell him exactly where I live because he might not understand why I'm doing this when home is such a big, fancy house. It would be embarrassing, so I tell him to drop me outside the train station, saying I've got to pick up some things from Tesco, because he probably thinks I'm way older than I am and living alone, or with mates, not still at home with my mum and dad. Besides, Mum would go apeshit if she saw me with an older man and climbing off the back of a motorbike. Tony doesn't question it; he just comes to a halt and gets off the bike. I do the same, taking off my helmet. He removes his too.

'We need to swap mobile numbers, partner.' He grins at me and airdrops me his. I do the same, and then he steps forwards and envelops me in a big hug. Oh God, he smells so good. He feels amazing. As he loosens his grip, I stand on tiptoes and lean in to kiss him because I'm sure he's just being restrained. But he turns his head away, and my lips meet his rough cheek.

Shit. I got that wrong.

'Hey, pretty Rose,' he says, obviously sensing my embarrassment. 'As much as I'd like to, I can't. I never mix work and pleasure. Never. And we're partners. Work partners, alright?'

My cheeks are flaming now, and he looks amused. He slips his hand out of his gloves and gives my cheek a little pinch, just like Grandad used to do when I was little.

'Don't worry, sweet Rose. You and me have got a great future ahead. I'll call you, alright?'

I watch as he climbs back onto his bike, and with a roar, he's gone.

That was the best afternoon of my life. Ever. I've got a partner, and whilst I screwed up a bit by trying to kiss him, he was kind of cool about it. I skip all the way home because this is my new beginning, and it's frigging awesome.

11

SIMONE

I've just returned from dropping Florian and Rose at school and am tidying up the things from breakfast, which probably isn't part of the concierge job description, but it's not like I can leave the kitchen looking like a bomb has hit.

Goldie appears looking as if she's barely slept. I can't help but feel sorry for her.

'I've got a terrible migraine,' she admits. 'But I can't afford to be ill. I'm meeting with potential investors later.'

And then she hurries out of the room, and I hear her throwing up. She's really suffering.

I'M WORKING through her inbox of emails when one pops in from the children's school, entitled *Rose Delucci – urgent*.

It's a message from the headteacher stating that due to Rose's poor attendance at school, unless she shows some serious application, they're going to have to ask her to leave. I go to find Goldie, because this is definitely a parent issue and not something I can resolve, but she's not in her study. I walk upstairs to Braun and Goldie's bedroom and gently knock on the door.

'Yes.'

I open the door. The curtains are closed, and Goldie is lying on the bed, fully clothed, a wet flannel over her eyes.

'Oh, I'm sorry to bother you,' I say.

She lifts the flannel off. 'It's alright. What's up?'

'You've had an email from Rose's school about her lack of attendance.'

Goldie sighs. 'Honestly, I don't know what to do about Rose. Perhaps she'll listen to you, the new face around here? Can you have a word with her?'

I don't think that I'm the right person at all, but I can hardly say no to Goldie seeing her lying like that on her bed, clearly suffering.

'Is there anything I can bring you?' I ask.

'You're so kind, Simone,' Goldie says. 'I don't know what I'd do without you. I've got to get rid of this migraine because I need to leave in half an hour to go to a meeting and won't be back until around 5.30 pm.'

As I shut the door, I feel bad that Goldie is going to have to cope without me and a lot sooner than she realises. If I don't uncover any interesting information about the Deluccis soon, I will have to accept I was barking up the wrong tree and get back to my normal life.

Thirty minutes later, Goldie appears in the kitchen. She's wearing a coat and leather boots, but she looks terribly pale.

'How's your head?' I ask.

She clutches it. 'Not great. Is there any chance you could drive me to my meeting? It's over in Soho. I'll get a cab home.'

'Of course,' I say. I nip downstairs to my flat and grab my coat and handbag. We take the Volkswagen, which I'm grateful for, as I wouldn't want to drive Goldie's car. The traffic is light, and after a few minutes, Goldie turns to me.

'I'm worried about Rose. I'd always hoped for a harmonious relationship with my daughter, but it seems I don't understand teenagers.'

'We forget what we were like at that age, don't we?'

'Uh-huh, not that I had a normal adolescence. Life was a lot tougher for me than it is for my kids.'

I glance at Goldie, but she's now gazing out of the passenger window. If only I could find out more about her, but I must remember that this is a strange employer-employee relationship.

Goldie breaks the silence. 'It just seems that the young question authority so much more today. Rose comes across as entitled. I know we've spoiled the kids, which is my fault because I've tried to give them everything that I didn't have, but I feel like I've screwed up.'

'Oh, Goldie, you haven't,' I say. 'Rose is pushing the boundaries, trying to find herself. That's what all young people do.'

And then her phone rings, and for the rest of the journey she's discussing budgets, timescales, and ways to reduce costs. There's a shift in my feelings towards Goldie. She's just like so many other working mothers, trying to juggle it all. I certainly don't get the sense that she's a bad person.

I PRINT off the email from the headteacher, and as soon as Rose steps into the house, I'm ready to accost her.

'I need a word with you, please,' I say.

'No time right now.' She barges past me and runs nimbly up the staircase. I follow her.

'You need to listen, Rose. Your parents have received an email from your school saying you'll be chucked out if you don't start attending classes.'

'Good,' she says, pulling off her school uniform with brazen disregard for me.

'It's not good, Rose. If you're chucked out of school, you won't get your A levels, which means you won't be going to university and you won't get a decent job. You're in danger of totally destroying your future.'

She turns to me, wearing just her bra and knickers, and I see that she has a belly button piercing and a large tattoo on her thigh.

'It's none of your bloody business, is it? Butt out of my life.'

'Your mother has asked me to talk to you.'

Rose turns her back to me and tugs on a black sweater and black leggings, jamming her feet into old black trainers.

'It's got nothing to do with you, so please just piss off,' she says.

'You don't get to talk to me like that!' I say, unable to hide the fury in my voice. 'I may be employed by your parents, but I'm not–' I don't get the chance to finish my sentence because she literally pushes past me and storms off down the stairs.

'Rose!' I shout after her. 'Where are you going?'

But she ignores me, and a second later the front door slams shut.

A COUPLE OF HOURS LATER, Goldie is home, but there's no sign of Rose. I tried ringing her mobile phone, but she has it switched off.

Goldie looks a little better, with some colour in her cheeks, and for the first time in ages she sits down at the kitchen table next to Florian and asks how he's getting on with his homework and whether he needs any help. The boy looks startled.

'How did you get on with Rose?' Goldie asks. I explain

that she stormed out of the house. Goldie looks livid. However, it isn't until two hours later, when Rose deems to return, I see the full force of Goldie's fury. She lets rip with Rose.

'You're a selfish, entitled girl who has no understanding of the importance of education.'

Rose just stands there, her arms crossed over her chest, a look of utter disinterest, as if the words are literally bouncing off her skin.

'Give me your debit card,' Goldie says, holding out her hand.

'Why?' Rose asks.

'Because grounding you obviously isn't enough. You won't have any spending money either, not for the foreseeable future.'

Rose smirks and, to my surprise, hands over the card.

There's something not right with this scenario, but I can't work out what's going on.

12

SIMONE

That evening, I think through the little I've found out about the Deluccis. There was something about Martin that didn't sit right with me. Perhaps it was the way he was so defensive when I asked questions about the night Ally died. I decide to do some more investigating into him and start off by looking up the films he's edited. He had huge success twenty years ago, working on one hit movie after another, and then there's a whole decade where he did nothing. That's odd. I search online, but I find absolutely nothing about him until last year, when his name pops up in a few press releases about him working with the Deluccis. It's weird. I consider calling Kit, but I doubt he'd know, firstly because Kit is too young, and secondly, how much do actors know about the behind-the-scenes guys?

I walk back upstairs to the main house, where I've put a chicken casserole in the slow cooker, ready for the Deluccis' supper. Goldie didn't ask me to, but as she's been out all day and had such a bad migraine this morning, I thought it would be the kind thing to do.

She's standing near the stove, clutching a folder of papers.

'Did you do this?' she asks, pointing at the slow cooker on the countertop.

I nod.

'That's so thoughtful of you. Why don't you join us for supper?'

I hesitate, because I haven't had supper with the family since that first night. But why not? It could result in some more insights.

ROSE IS in a foul mood and doesn't say a word although she does throw daggers at me from time to time. It's hardly my fault her mother took her debit card, so I just stare back at her. She doesn't know how to deal with that so keeps her eyes on her food from then on. Florian is a little brighter this evening, perhaps because Goldie spent some time with him. Braun hasn't tipped up.

'He'll have forgotten what the time is,' Goldie says lightly. 'When he's in the editing suite, he loses track of everything in the real world.' She sends him a text message.

'How's the editing going on your new film?' I ask as Goldie fills up all of our glasses of water.

'Good, but that's Braun's domain.'

'He was here with his editor a few days ago.' It's a risk mentioning this in Rose's presence, but she doesn't say anything. I think she's got the measure of me.

'Ah yes, Martin. At this point in the film, they spend all their time together.'

'How do you choose an editor?'

'We needed someone really good but not too expensive. They're hard to come by.'

'If he's so good, how come he's cheap?'

She hesitates for a moment. 'He was away from the industry for a number of years.'

'Oh, a career break?' I ask, trying to sound casual.

'Not exactly. Martin was and is a very talented editor. He worked on high-profile movies, but he began to drink too much. The alcoholism affected his work, and then the work dried up. He didn't work on films for a long time, but he sorted his personal life, stopped drinking and was desperate to get back into editing again. Braun gave him this break, and by all accounts, he's doing a great job.'

'Just an old soak,' Rose mutters under her breath. Florian sniggers, and Goldie says, 'Neither of you repeat a word of what I just said, alright?'

And then Braun walks in. The atmosphere changes instantly. Goldie jumps up and gives him a kiss.

'Hiya, all,' he says, sitting heavily on the chair opposite his wife. 'What's new?'

The children don't answer. 'How was your day, love?' Goldie asks him.

'Good. You might be interested in our next film, Florian,' Braun says. 'It's about a history of art student and the professor she marries. Her flatmate disappeared when she was at uni, and then years later, a TV researcher tips up wanting to investigate what happened to her friend. It's set in the world of art.'

'Florian likes anime, Dad. Not old masters.'

'I'm not really sure the storyline is appropriate for someone of Florian's age.' Goldie laughs, patting Florian on the shoulder. The boy says nothing.

'Anyway, I want to start casting. I'm thinking Brendan Fernsby for the male lead and Sabrina Caccionella for the female lead.'

'Brendan Fernsby is lush,' Rose says.

'He's old enough to be your father.' Goldie scowls.

'So?' Rose replies, clearly looking for a fight.

Even I have heard of those two Hollywood actors.

'I want to audition candidates for the two leads,' Braun says.

Goldie frowns. 'But we haven't even briefed the casting agent yet, and you can't start auditioning until we've got the finance in place.'

Braun huffs and swishes his hand to one side. 'What's the harm in getting started, getting ahead a little? Let's get going.'

'No, Braun,' Goldie says.

I notice that Florian's shoulders tense while Rose seems to be totally ignoring her parents' conversation.

'You can't cast for a part with people as high profile as Brendan Fernsby and Sabrina Caccionella and then the parts don't materialise. Imagine how damaging that would be for our reputation. We're a new and upcoming production house; it would ruin us.'

'Why wouldn't the parts materialise?' Braun asks.

'If we don't raise the money.' Goldie toys with the remaining food on her plate and then places her knife and fork over it.

Braun lets out a guffaw. 'There's no chance we won't get the funding, is there?'

Goldie doesn't say anything.

Braun asks again. 'Is there?'

He still doesn't get an answer, so I butt in and ask if anyone would like more food. There's something uncomfortable about this dialogue, almost as if no one in this family is on the same wavelength. I'm glad when the meal is over.

IT ISN'T until later that I fully absorb Goldie's words from our discussions earlier in the day. If Braun gave Martin such a big break, then the editor is going to be very loyal to Braun. It makes sense that he was uncomfortable with my probing. It also suggests that I'm unlikely to get the truth out of him. I need to talk to other members of the cast who were there when they wrapped filming the night of Ally's death, but who, and how? And then it strikes me. What about visiting the location? What if it wasn't just a member of the crew or cast who saw Ally leave that evening. What if there is CCTV and I can get access to it somehow?

I TOSS and turn all night, wondering whether the location might hold some answers for me. And then when dawn breaks and a pale grey light filters in through the curtains, I take out my phone and search for the film studio location of *The Insomniac*. It's easy to find, listed on a website that features information about British films.

Oakline Film Studios is on an industrial estate on the far fringes of northwest London. It's not somewhere easily accessible by public transport, so my visit is going to require a bit of planning.

In the morning, I ask Goldie if I could have a day off midweek in exchange for working a Sunday, and she readily agrees. Now I just have to be patient.

TWO DAYS LATER, I get up early and walk to East Putney, where I rent a car for the day, an anonymous Prius. I could have taken the electric Golf that is available for my use, but somehow that feels wrong, and besides, I wouldn't want the car to be recognised there. I follow the directions on my phone, and it's much further than I assumed, out beyond the metropolis. I drive through a wooded area and realise that it could be any one of these trees that took Ally's life. I haven't been to the location where she died. Even though the police pointed out the exact spot on a map, I just couldn't bring myself to go there. I understand why people may choose to leave flowers and mark the spot of the death of their loved ones, but it's not for me. I shiver.

It's no surprise that Ally was exhausted because having to come here every day was a monumental commute to work. And then I'm speared by grief. It hits me in my solar plexus, and the tears come so rapidly, I have to pull the car over into a bus stop. For several minutes the sobs rack through me, and I realise that I haven't properly grieved. Yes, I've cried. Of course I've felt desolate, empty and sad, but I've tried to stuff the real emotion deep inside while focusing on the events surrounding Ally's death. My time with the Deluccis has been so practical, I've blocked out true feelings. It takes a while, but when I've pulled myself together enough to drive, I wipe my eyes, dab some concealer on my red nose and start the car. I force myself to focus on the miniscule positive, that at least Ally was spending her last days in a leafy location.

But five minutes later those thoughts are dashed. The satnav on my phone leads me to an industrial estate, an anonymous place that could be anywhere in the country. I suppose I had thought that filming might take place in an exotic location; I'm disappointed. Green trees give way to large, squat buildings, the premises of companies ranging from paint wholesalers to a bakery. The film studio is in unit 34c and is a triple-height, large shed-like building painted white with two huge, grey corrugated iron openings, I assume so articulated lorries can easily offload. Outside there is a large parking area, empty today except for two cars and a white transit van. As I get out of the car and look around, I see several CCTV cameras on the exterior of the building. For a moment, I hesitate. What am I doing here? Will I be caught on those cameras, and does that matter? It's very unlikely anyone will tell me anything; besides, isn't CCTV footage wiped every few weeks? But I haven't come this far and had the expense of renting a car without at least stepping foot inside the place. I walk up to the front door and try to turn the handle. It's locked. I notice a small intercom on the wall, so I press the buzzer.

'Hello.' The man's voice sounds muffled.

'Um, I work for Braun Delucci. Wondering if I could have a word.'

'Wait a moment. I'll be down.'

I stand outside the door, quickly thinking through my story. About a minute later, the door swings open, and a security guard steps out. A tall, sturdy bloke with a shiny, bald head, he has a bunch of keys attached to his belt, making him look like a prison warden.

'How can I help?'

'Sorry to disturb you, but I'm Braun Delucci's personal assistant. He's lost a pair of very expensive designer sunglasses, and I was wondering whether they might have been left here. Has he been here the last few days?'

The guard frowns, and I can't decide if he processes things slowly or whether he sees right through my ruse. Eventually he replies, 'No, I don't think I've seen Mr Delucci here for a while, not since they wrapped filming.'

'Oh. I was sure he said I should check here. Do you think I could take a quick look around anyway? It's just that you know what these film directors are like. My job will be on the line if I don't find them.' I roll my eyes. 'I mean, it's ridiculous over a pair of sunglasses, but you know how it is. He's convinced they've been stolen, but he's probably just misplaced them.'

I feel a twinge of guilt for suggesting that Braun is like this, because as much as I don't want to like him, he hasn't treated me badly. Then again, I've barely had any contact with him.

'What? He's suggesting someone here has nicked them?' The guard pulls his chin inwards and crosses his arms.

'No, not specifically.' I'm floundering. 'I noticed you've got CCTV. Is it worth checking them?'

'Nah. They're external cameras only.'

'How long are the recordings kept for?'

He scowls at me, and I realise I'm pushing my luck.

'Sorry, lady, but I'm not going through the recordings for a pair of bloody sunglasses. Anyway, they're written over every fortnight.'

'You're right, stupid idea. But if you come across them, would you mind letting me know.'

He sighs but takes out his phone. I recite my mobile number, changing the last digit.

'Thanks for your help, sir,' I say deferentially. I turn and walk away slowly, waiting for the door to close behind him. That was a waste of time, but I'm not ready to give up yet. Just because the security guard doesn't want to let me in doesn't mean I'm not going to scour the place. I double back on myself and walk briskly down the left-hand side of the building. There are two doors on this side. The first is a fire door. I try it, but it's locked. After a bank of dumpster bins there is a second door and a sign on it that says Staff Only. It's also locked. I carry on walking, but as I do so, I hear the door open, so I turn around. A man appears wearing dark blue overalls that stretch tightly over his rounded belly. He's pulling an overflowing black bin. After tipping the contents of the bin into one of the dumpsters, he rummages in his pocket and produces a cigarette and lighter. I turn around and walk towards him.

'Sorry to disturb you, but do you work here?'

He nods, letting out a ring of smoke.

'I work for the Deluccis. Do you know them?'

'Yeah. They were here for months, filming. Only left recently. Why?'

'Braun Delucci has lost a pair of expensive sunglasses, and this is one of the places I'm checking out.' I take a step nearer and lower the tone of my voice so it sounds conspiratorial. 'As I said to your colleague, the security guard, I'm sure he'll have left them on the table of a restaurant, or they fell out of the car. But I'm new to the job, so I've got to do what he says.'

'Yeah. A bit gobby that one.'

I laugh.

'Kept them working all hours. I had to work overtime, which was fine by me, as I need the dosh, but still.'

'It must be interesting getting to know all the famous film people,' I suggest.

He harrumphs. 'The people here aren't famous. C-listers at best. Besides, I'm invisible to most of them. There's the odd nice person. It was terrible the way that shoot ended though.'

'What do you mean?' I try to keep my face impassive.

'That poor actress died the last night of filming. She was one of the nice ones.'

'Oh yes. It was tragic. So you were here that evening?' I mentally cross my fingers in the hope that this janitor will give me the information I need.

'Yes.' He takes a deep inhale of his cigarette.

'Did you see her leave?'

'Yes, she and Braun Delucci, they left together. It was raining that night. I'd come out for a smoke and saw them running across the car park in the rain.'

I open and close my mouth because I'm really not sure what to say to that, but I could hug this man. He's just confirmed what I've always known deep down. Ally wouldn't have taken Goldie's car without the Deluccis' permission.

'Did they leave together?' I ask.

'I think so, but it was tipping it down cats and dogs, so I went back inside. Can't be sure, you know. Terrible what happened to her. So young and pretty.'

'Did the police talk to you about what you saw that evening?'

'Nah. I'm just one of the janitors, a nobody. I hung around for a couple of hours after my shift ended to drink beers with the crew. And then a couple of days later, I got Covid and was off work for a few weeks.'

'Right,' I say, glancing at my watch. 'I need to check out the next place on the list. All the best.'

But as I get into the hire car, my initial euphoria quickly dissipates. All I have is the janitor's word that they might have left together. Braun could have shown Ally how the car worked and then returned inside. I have no evidence. If I go to the police with that little titbit, they're just going to think I'm crazy. There's a lot more digging that needs to be done.

As I'm driving back to the car rental place, Rob calls.

'Simone,' and then his voice cracks.

'What's happened?' I ask, panic immediately flooding my veins.

'Nothing. I just wanted to hear a friendly voice.' Something isn't right, so I indicate and pull over into a lay-by.

'What's going on? Tell me how you are?' I ask.

'Been better.' His voice quivers.

'Of course you have. We're all broken. How's Carly?'

And then Rob sobs. 'I'm sorry, Simone, but I'm not coping. I just can't live without her. I don't sleep, and then I'm short with Carly, and she deserves so much more. My doctor gave me antidepressants, but they're not working, and I've got to sort myself out.'

'Oh, Rob,' I say, realising how difficult it must be for him to even admit how hard he's grieving. 'What can I do to help?'

'Do you think you could have Carly for a week or so just to give me the chance to get my head together? I can't ask Mum and Dad to do any more. They're exhausted and need a break too.'

'Of course,' I say and then realise that Rob thinks I'm at home, doing my bookkeeping, in charge of my own destiny. But I'm not. I have a live-in position, and if he knew it was at the Deluccis' house... 'I've got rather a lot on,' I say. 'Let me get back to you later. Is that okay?'

'Sure.'

How am I going to juggle this one? I love little Carly, and under normal circumstances, there's nothing I'd want more than to look after her, but how will it work at the Deluccis? I can hardly ask for a week off when I've only just started working there, and now I have evidence, however intangible, that Braun left with Ally that night, I can't possibly leave. I'm going to have to speak to Goldie and come up with some story.

GOLDIE IS IN THE KITCHEN, her phone wedged underneath her ear, stirring a pan on the stove with one hand and reading something on her iPad with the other. Talk about multitasking. I wait until she's off the phone before clearing my throat.

'Um, can I do anything to help?'

'No, I'm fine, thanks.' And then I wonder whether perhaps Goldie likes being so frenetically busy, whether perhaps she's running away from something, juggling crazily to avoid having time to sit with her troubling thoughts. But am I reading something into Goldie's life just because I don't trust her husband?

'I've got a slightly awkward situation,' I say, and then I stop myself just in time. I mustn't let Goldie know that Carly's mother died; otherwise she might – however unlikely it is – put two and two together. On the other hand, I can't stop little Carly from letting slip that her mummy has gone to heaven. Goldie turns to look at me, an eyebrow raised.

'My brother and sister-in-law have recently split up. Actually, my sister-in-law has walked out and said she's not coming back, and they've got a four-year-old daughter. My brother isn't coping very well, and he's asked if I could look after Carly for a week whilst he tries to pull himself together. I know this is totally out of line, but is there any possibility Carly might be able to stay with me here? I'll make sure that she's at nursery in the day and that it doesn't detract from my work.' And then I wonder. Will Goldie recognise the name Carly because it's not that common a name? But how likely was it that Ally mentioned her daughter's name? Probably very unlikely because I know how professional Ally was trying to be. She'd told me how she had to pretend she didn't have a family life because commitment to her career was essential.

There's a moment's hesitation when I'm sure that Goldie is going to say no, but instead she puts the wooden spoon into the pan and turns to fully face me.

'Oh, that's terrible, Simone. Of course you can have her to stay. I love little children. Goodness, how have you explained the disappearance of her mother to Carly?'

'We've told her that her mummy has gone to heaven. It was the easiest explanation because how else can you tell a young child that their mother has deserted them?'

Goldie gasps, and I wonder if I've gone too far with the explanation.

'I know it's a dramatic explanation, but her mother is a drug taker, and she's not coming back, so we just thought it was easier this way.'

'I suppose you're right,' Goldie muses. 'It'll be lovely to have a little person around the house again.'

I smile, relieved. Even so, I know that I'm going to have to be very careful.

13

GOLDIE

Simone really is a godsend. Nothing is too much trouble for her, and there's none of the tutting or eye-rolling I got from Lauren. She's organised, she deals with my emails without coming to me questioning every tiny thing, and she even tried to sort out Rose without hassling me. Not that anyone can achieve that. Tonight, Braun and I are out to an art exhibition, and she even offered to babysit Florian. I feel like a weight has been lifted off my shoulders, allowing me to put all my energy into organising things for our next film. I have about half the funding already secured, so now I need to sign contracts for the studio space. Against my better judgement, I gave in to Braun's pestering and agreed to let him start auditioning for *What She Knew*.

Today, I'm going back to the studio we rented for *The Insomniac*. The next film will need a larger space, but I'm hoping to secure it for the same price as the last one. We'll see.

I drive the familiar route to the studios, listening to audition pieces by various actors, even though I think Braun is being premature in starting the process. I know it's ultimately

Braun's decision as the director who to cast, but he'll take on board my opinions if I strongly dislike an audition. On the whole, we work well together. The ones I like, I'll view on the big television screen at home, and then it's over to Braun to do the live auditions. It's raining as I pull into the car park, so I grab my umbrella and hurry to the front door.

Will, the security guard, opens the door before I even press the buzzer. 'Good morning, Mrs Delucci,' he says, stepping to one side to let me in. I've told him to call me Goldie on numerous occasions, but he still persists on being formal.

'How are you, Will?'

'Enjoying the quiet. Filming starts again next week, and it'll be hectic. What about you? What are your plans?'

'I'm here to meet with Ethan to discuss contracts for the next one.'

'That's good.' We walk companionably along the corridor, which is lined with photographs of many of the leading British actors from the past decade.

'Oh, by the way, did Mr Delucci find his sunglasses?'

I stop walking. 'Sorry?'

'His personal assistant was here looking for them. Said Mr Delucci had lost some designer sunglasses.'

'What, Lauren was here?'

'No, not Lauren. The new lady. What's her name?'

'Simone?'

'That's the one.'

I'm stumped for words because firstly I didn't know Braun had lost his glasses, and secondly, why would he send Simone here when Braun hasn't been to the studios for the past few weeks. And would he really send Simone all the way out here just for a pair of sunglasses? He's been working in the editing suite with Martin. It doesn't make sense.

But I don't have time to think about it because Ethan steps out of his office, his hand outstretched. He's mid-fifties, hair shaved so short it's barely visible, and his biceps are so large, they're probably not much smaller than my waist. He's a short guy who, I've noticed, wears trainers with extra deep soles, probably to give him more height.

'Good to see you, Goldie.' He ushers me inside, the annoying sound of him chewing gum already grating.

'So, film number three,' he says, sucking on the gum.

'We're nearly there on the funding, so it's time to tie up the logistical things. We'd like to rent your studios again, but we'll need studio two this time, as the sets will be larger.'

'I'm sure that can be organised.' He passes the rate card over the table.

'Ah, come on, Ethan. We're a loyal customer, coming back for more. I need you to offer us studio two for the price of studio three.'

'No can do.' He shakes his head.

'Why not? You're not even fully booked. There's no one in here this week.'

'The diary is looking extremely full. If I give in to you, I have to give in to the next production company.'

'I know you do discounts for Telepent Productions.'

'They don't have the same sort of problems.'

'Problems?'

'Look, Goldie, there are a lot of rumours going around about the amount of drugs on set on *The Insomniac*, that things weren't really under control. I can't have that sort of stuff going on here. If the police raid the place, that's our business gone for ever.'

I have no response to this. What has Ethan heard about drugs on set?

'Do you have any actual proof of drugs during our filming? Did you see it yourself?' I ask, sitting up straighter in my chair.

He shakes his head.

'So it's the gossip mill. Surely you don't listen to that.' I'm also annoyed that the PR company hasn't eliminated the rumour. I'll need to have words with them too.

'Look, we'll have you back with pleasure, but you're going to have to pay full whack. And clean up the drugs, okay?'

'The only person we know who took drugs was Alison Greystone. There is nothing to suggest it was endemic.'

'Sorry, Goldie, but that's the way it is.'

This conversation isn't over with, and if I need to find another studio, then I will.

'I hear you,' I say, standing up.

Ethan hands me a sheaf of papers, which I know is the standard contract. I won't be signing it.

'Good to see you again, Goldie,' he says.

I smile tightly because I don't feel the same way.

I'M JUST GETTING onto the North Circular when my phone rings. It's Florian, announced by the music for *Doctor Who*, put on my phone as his unique ringtone by Rose. It annoys Florian now, who is very much over his *Doctor Who* phase.

'Darling,' I say.

'Where are you, Mum?'

I pause for a moment because where should I be other than here?

'The music competition starts in five minutes, and everyone else's parents are here. You said you'd be here,' he whines.

'Oh God, Florian. Yes, I'll be there as quickly as I can. And in the unlikely event I don't make it in time to hear you play, good luck, sweetheart.'

He hangs up on me. My little boy actually hung up on me, and I don't even blame him. How the hell could I forget? We talked about it this morning at breakfast. Simone even pulled me to one side after Florian had gone upstairs to brush his teeth to ask if I'd like her to go instead because my diary was so jam-packed, but I said no. I promised I'd make it. And now I have five minutes to make a journey that with no traffic normally takes thirty-five minutes.

It's absolute crap when women say they can have it all. It's just not possible because time is limited, however organised we try to be, however much we rally support and delegate. Attention can only truly be given to one thing at a time, and for too long, my attention has been on Delucci Productions and not my children. I call Braun.

'Hey, love. How quickly can you get to the kids' school?'

'Why, what's happened?'

'I'm going to be late for Florian's music competition, and I promised I'd be there. Can you step in?'

'Ergh, no, Goldie!' Braun says, his voice cutting with sarcasm. 'I have a film to edit, and it's you who reminds me about the deadlines and the budgets every single day. I'm working my balls off here.'

You're not the only one, I think. And I do everything at home, make sure that the family is fed, birthday presents are bought, bills are paid, and social events are attended. A surge of resentment sweeps through me, and I hang up on my husband just as Florian did to me. Perhaps I should ring Simone and get her to go to the school, as she's the nearest, but it's not fair on Florian. He barely knows Simone. Instead, I put my foot down on the accelerator. I'll deal with the speeding tickets if I have to. It doesn't escape me that this was how Ally died, by driving too fast. I kid myself that I'll be fine because she was driving on a rainy night with her body full of meth, whereas today the sun is shining, and all I've taken today is a paracetamol.

I race through London's streets, and I'm sure that I'm flashed by speed cameras at least twice. Near the school, there's nowhere to park, so I leave the car on a single yellow line and just pray it isn't clamped or removed by the time I return. I run to the school gates and repeatedly press on the buzzer. By the time I'm shown into the school theatre (and yes, it does have a proper theatre, being a very expensive, fee-paying private school with the finest of facilities), there are no seats left. I stand at the back and am met with a tut from a teacher. The next child on the stage is a young girl, her knees trembling as she brings the flute to her lips and stares with watery eyes at the teacher accompanying her at the piano.

'Excuse me, where are we up to?' I whisper to the teacher, who glowers at me before handing me a copy of the programme and pointing to about two-thirds down the list of performers. My heart sinks. I have to use the light from my mobile phone to read it, which evokes another tut from the teacher, but just as the audience stops applauding the young flautist, who despite her fear did a remarkably good job, the head of music speaks through the microphone.

'Our next contestant is Florian Delucci on the clarinet.' The applause is a bit muted, but I am so relieved to be here in time, I jump up and down, waving my arms in the hope that Florian can see me through the glare of the stage lights.

Despite my boy being painfully shy and struggling at school, he is musically gifted. The piece isn't difficult, but he plays it flawlessly, and even the miserable teacher standing next to me mutters, 'Very good,' under her breath.

Florian comes fourth in his section. I know he'll be disappointed, but he's still so young and new to this school, and I'm immensely proud of him. After the winners have been presented with their cups and certificates, the children are allowed ten minutes with their parents and guardians. I weave my way to the front of the theatre as the children come out, eventually spotting Florian walking alone, his head down.

'You were amazing, darling!' I say, throwing my arms around him. He immediately wriggles free. 'Congratulations.'

'I thought you weren't going to be here.'

'I wouldn't miss you playing for anything. You know that. I'm so proud of you.'

'But you nearly did,' Florian says, crossing his arms. 'I saw you come in.'

'I made it in time, though, and that was the most important thing. What would you like as a treat for doing so well?'

He scowls at me. 'I didn't do so well. I came fourth.'

'In my book that was amazing. Faultless. And next year you'll probably win your section.'

'Can you watch a film with me tonight?'

'Oh, darling, I can't tonight. Dad and I have to go out, and Simone is babysitting. Tomorrow night maybe?'

His face closes down. 'Whatever. Need to go now.' He turns away from me, his shoulders slumped, and my heart cracks at the pain my boy is suffering. I want to go after him, scoop him up and take him home right now, but then a bell rings, and all the kids leave their parents, and I lose sight of Florian in amongst the taller children.

A few hours later, I'm getting ready for the art exhibition. Frankly, I could do without going, as I've no interest in buying any paintings, but it's an event organised by a London-based film investment fund, and as we screwed up the meeting with the Americans, this one is very important. I'm wearing a charcoal grey dress that fits like a glove and a chunky gold necklace, a statement piece that I bought myself when we signed the deal for *The Insomniac*. I slip into my high-heeled shoes.

'You look gorgeous,' Braun says as he appears out of the bathroom. That's the thing with my husband. He remembers to compliment me, he notices me, and I know that's unusual.

Most of my girlfriends admit their husbands wouldn't notice if they came home with their hair in a buzz cut.

'Thanks, so do you,' I say on automaton. And then I really look at him. Braun is wearing a starched white shirt, open-necked, a dark blazer and tightly cut trousers, but on top of his head are his sunglasses.

'So you found them, then?'

'Found what?'

'The sunglasses. I gather you sent Simone to the studios to look for them.'

He frowns. 'What are you talking about? I haven't lost my glasses.'

Now it's my turn to be confused. Surely Will, the janitor, wouldn't have got Braun mixed up with anyone else, yet he specifically said that Simone was at the studios.

'Apparently Simone went looking for them.' And then the doorbell rings.

'The taxi,' Braun says. 'We'd better go.'

A few moments later, we're sitting in the cab on the way to the Mayfair art gallery.

'It's weird about Simone going to the studios,' I say. 'I hope she doesn't let us down like Lauren.'

'She's nothing like Lauren,' Braun says, his voice lower and tighter than normal. I glance at him, but he's staring out of the window, his head turned away from me. 'Right, tell me who's who this evening and what I'm meant to be saying.'

But it's hard to concentrate on the evening ahead. The situation with Simone makes me feel uncomfortable and disappointed. The last thing I want to do is to have to replace her. Everything seems to be running so smoothly at home. And then I remember. I still haven't issued Simone with her employment contract and non-disclosure agreement. I really must do that tomorrow.

14

SIMONE

Florian seems particularly despondent. After school, he goes straight up to his room, and when I pop up to check on him, he is sitting there, his schoolbooks open in front of him, tears dripping down his face.

'Hey,' I say, hurrying into the room. 'What's up?'

He quickly wipes his cheeks. 'Nothing,' he replies, but his voice is choked up.

'How are you doing with your homework?' I perch on the end of his bed.

'I can't do it,' he says quietly. 'I'm really thick and don't get any of it. The only thing I can do is music, and even in that I only came fourth.'

'Fourth!' I exclaim. 'I never came fourth in anything. More like fortieth. Struggling at school means absolutely nothing.'

'I could tell that Mum was really disappointed in me.'

I have no idea what Goldie feels, but I reach forwards and take his hand. 'Your mum told me how proud she is of you. And so am I.' I'm not sure that counts for anything, but it doesn't harm to say it. Florian smiles weakly.

'How about you and me playing a game or doing something nice this evening. What do you reckon?'

'There's a film I'd like to watch.'

'Perfect. Why don't you finish your homework? We'll have tea, and then we'll settle down to watch it together.'

'Thank you, Simone,' he says, and he looks at me with such gratitude that I feel an overwhelming desire to hug this lost soul of a boy who isn't mine. I hurry out of the room before I make things awkward for both of us. It makes me think of Carly, who is growing up without a mother and what a terrible loss it will be for her. And with that thought I feel a frustration that I still don't know exactly what happened on the evening of Ally's death.

A COUPLE OF HOURS LATER, we're sitting in the living room, watching some cartoon-type film on a giant television screen.

'Can you pause a moment?' I ask Florian. 'I need to pop to the loo.'

As I'm walking into the hall, I run straight into Rose. She's wearing skintight leather trousers and a biker's jacket with a white crop top underneath.

'Where are you going?' I ask.

'Out.'

'No you're not, young lady. Your mother specifically said you're to stay here this evening and do your schoolwork.'

Rose ignores me and types with two thumbs into her phone.

'Rose, I'm talking to you.'

'And I'm not listening,' she says, without looking up.

'Look, I don't want to get into an argument, and I don't make up the rules around here, but you know you're not allowed to go out on a school night.'

'My friend is here and waiting for me. I've got to go.'

I stride to the front door and lock it, then stand in front of it.

'You're not going anywhere on my watch without your parents' permission. You know perfectly well that your mother has grounded you during the week. Do not back me into a corner, Rose.'

'You're not my prison guard,' she says. 'I can do whatever I like.'

'I'm sorry, but the answer is no. I'm following your parents' instructions, and you know that you're not allowed out.'

'You're just like the last bitch, aren't you?' she yells at me. But to my relief, she turns around and runs up the stairs, slamming her bedroom door so loudly the whole house shudders.

I sigh and walk towards the window next to the front door. There's a man standing in the entranceway to the drive, leaning against a bright red motorbike, smoking a cigarette. He's wearing black leathers, and when he looks up, I'm surprised to see how old he is. He must be early thirties at least, much too old for Rose. I wonder whether her parents know that she's hanging around with a man who is nearly double her age. Oh, Rose, I think to myself. What have you got yourself into? I continue on to the bathroom, and when I'm done, I walk slowly back into the living room because the Deluccis' children are really not my problem. I just have a soft spot for Florian.

By 10 PM, Florian is asleep, and Rose is shut away inside her bedroom. At least I hope she is. There's loud music playing in her room, the heavy beat thumping into the hall. I've done as much snooping as I can, but when Rose said that I was a bitch like Lauren, it got me thinking. Lauren is the obvious person to pump for information. We had a rapport when we met, and now the time has come to get back in touch.

I send her a text message, and despite it being late, she responds immediately, suggesting we meet for a coffee tomorrow.

I run myself a bath and use just one drop of scented oil. Ally gave me the bottle of bath oil for my birthday, and I'm trying to eke it out for as long as I can. I sink into the bath and think. What am I doing here? I've put my life on hold and become a skivvy to the Delucci family, and for what? It's like I don't have a normal life anymore. I don't go out, I don't meet up with friends, I'm not interested in having a love life, and I'm not even working on my business. I wonder if perhaps deep down I feel like I don't deserve a normal life; I don't deserve happiness until I can get to the bottom of what really happened to Ally. This has become such a single-minded quest for me, but have I got it all wrong? I've never seriously considered whether Ally might have been a drug addict. I thought I knew, Rob did too, but could she have hidden it from us? Could it have been a new thing, just since she was working on *The Insomniac*? I groan and add more hot water to the bath. No, I just can't see it. What are the alternatives? Perhaps she was having an affair with Braun, and that's why they left together. Maybe Ally was pregnant, and the child was Braun's not Rob's, and she'd threatened to tell Goldie. As a result, Braun tried to kill her. No, that's ridiculous. I'm getting melodramatic. Ally loved Rob. Besides, if Ally had been pregnant, that would have shown up at the autopsy.

And then I think about what Ally would say to me right now. It's as if I can hear her voice right here in this small bathroom. 'This isn't normal, Simone. What you're doing, the way you're living. It isn't right. You need to get back to your own life.'

I climb out of the bath. The voice in my head may be right, but I'm not ready to stop yet. Soon maybe, but not quite yet.

WE GREET each other with a kiss on the cheek and take our seats at a table near the back of the coffee shop.

'How are things?' I ask her.

'I'm doing some freelance work and am on the shortlist for a job with a family in Dubai. Keep your fingers crossed for me.'

'I will.'

'And you? What's the latest?'

I take a deep breath. I know this is risky, but unless I'm honest with Lauren, I don't see how I'm going to be able to dig deeper, to get information from her that might actually lead somewhere. 'I've got an admission to make.'

'Oh yes.' She tilts her head to one side.

'I've got your old job. I'm working with the Deluccis.'

Lauren's mouth drops open. 'You what?'

'I know it's a bit weird–'

'It's more than a bit weird. It's psycho like, Simone. We became friends, and then you get my job. How long have you been in it?'

'Three weeks,' I admit.

'Shit. Did you befriend me on purpose?' She pushes her chair away from the table as if she's going to flee, and frankly, I don't blame her. It does come across as freaky.

'No, it's nothing like that, Lauren. Please don't go. I need to tell you the truth.' I like Lauren, and I sense that despite this bombshell, she likes me. I need to trust her.

She looks at me warily, but she doesn't move.

'I hadn't planned it this way at all, but I did want to find out more about the Deluccis. Honestly, I never meant to get your job, and the friendship we've struck up, that's genuine, I promise. From my side at least. The thing is, I'm Alison Greystone's sister.'

Lauren stares at me, initially with incomprehension.

'Ally, the actress who died in the car accident in Goldie's car,' I explain.

Lauren looks really shocked, and I don't blame her.

'You managed to talk your way into the job, and they don't know who you really are?'

I nod.

'Shit, Simone. I'm impressed, girl.' Lauren grins at me and moves her chair back to the table.

'You are?' I say, feeling relieved.

'It takes guts to do that.'

'You see, I really need to find out more about Braun. I think he might have left with Ally that night, and there are various things that don't stack up. For starters, my sister never did drugs, but there were drugs found in her bloodstream.'

I can't work out Lauren's expression, but then she says, 'I'm sorry your sister died. It's horrible.' She smooths out the little biscuit wrapper that came free with her coffee.

'I was wondering if you might be able to tell me a bit more about the Deluccis. Do they do drugs?'

Lauren stares around the coffee shop, and for a moment, I wonder if she heard the question, but just as I'm about to repeat myself, she turns to look at me. 'No, I can't be one hundred per cent sure, but I never saw either of them do drugs.'

'Right.'

And then she pushes her empty coffee cup to the edge of the table and leans towards me. 'So tell me the goss. Is Rose a bitch to you too?'

'She's a handful, but I give as good as I get. Honestly, I'd expected to dislike them all, but I don't. I think Goldie is super stressed and overworked, and I've barely seen anything of Braun. What did you think of them?'

'That they treated me like a slave, and I'm glad not to be working there anymore. How's Florian?'

'Poor Florian. I feel sorry for him. Rose can stand up for herself, but Florian just seems lost.'

Lauren nods in agreement.

'Actually, I've got my niece coming to stay with me for a few days. I thought Goldie might object, but she's been really nice about it.'

'No surprise there. Goldie is lovely to all children except her own. She doesn't have time for them. She's a lousy mother.'

I'm inclined to agree with Lauren. Not because Goldie intends to be a bad mother, but she doesn't give her children the time they need. Rose is out of control, and Florian is lost.

We spend the next thirty minutes or so chatting about life, our hopes for the future and share some laughs about our experiences with the Deluccis. I don't learn anything new from Lauren, but it's still an enjoyable chat.

'Have you forgiven me?' I ask as we shrug our coats on.

'I still think it's a bit weird, but yes, I guess so,' she says with a smirk.

We agree to meet up again soon.

THE NEXT DAY, I go over to Rob and Ally's house to collect Carly.

I ring the doorbell and am about to ring it again when an upstairs window opens, and Rob leans out. 'It's open, Simone. Let yourself in.'

I dig my nails into the palm of my hand as I enter the

house. I can see why Rob is finding it so hard. Ally is everywhere in here; her coats are still hanging in the hallway; the
photos she chose are on the mantelpiece in the living room;
even her favourite mug is out on the countertop in the
kitchen next to the kettle. It's as if she's popped out for a
couple of hours and will be back any time soon. Except she
won't. Perhaps it would be better if Rob and Carly moved
house, yet I know I can't suggest that.

'Aunty Simmie!' Carly comes careering towards me,
throwing her arms around my legs. 'Is it true I'm coming to
stay?'

I bend down so I'm level with her. 'Would you like that?'

'Yaaas!' she says, throwing her arms around my shoulders.

'Have you packed your bag?'

'Daddy's packed it.' She then steps away from me and
with a very serious expression says, 'But I don't think he's
very good at it. Will you check everything's in it?'

'Of course I will.' She leads me by the hand, and we go
upstairs to her bedroom. I have to swallow hard because even
Ally's scent lingers up here. I'm not sure what perfume she
used, but it had undertones of citrus, a light scent just like
her. I wonder if Rob has been spraying it to keep her memory
alive.

'Hey,' he says as he steps out of Carly's room. He looks
terrible. He must have lost over a stone, he hasn't shaved in
days, and his eyes are bloodshot. He gives me a kiss on the
cheek, and I smell alcohol on his breath. Oh, Rob.

'It's not that we don't trust you,' I say, trying to keep my
voice light, 'but Carly and I just need to double-check what's
inside that suitcase.' I wink at Rob, and he tries very hard to
smile at me.

'Sure.'

A few minutes later, when I've got Carly's suitcase ready,
and we've carried it downstairs, I turn to the little girl. 'Can

you go and do a final double-check of your room and bathroom to make sure we've got everything you'll need?'

She runs up the stairs.

'I'm so sorry, Rob,' I say, throwing my arms around him. 'Will you be able to get the help you need?'

'Yes, I'll try,' he says gruffly. 'It's just I don't think I'll ever get over this. Ally was the love of my life, and I simply don't know how to exist without her.'

'I know. I miss her every second of every day. But you need to take care of yourself and get better for Carly's sake.' I glance at my watch. 'Our Uber will be here in a couple of minutes. I'll look after her, don't worry. You just take good care and go and see your doctor. Tell him the truth, Rob. Everything you're feeling, how you're not sleeping, and don't be angry with me, but I can smell the alcohol on your breath. It's understandable, Rob. But please get help.'

He nods at me, and I can tell that he's barely holding himself together. When I bundle Carly into the taxi, I turn to look at Rob. Tears are flowing down his cheeks into his ragged beard. My heart breaks all over again.

'Why aren't we going to your house?' Carly asks as we stand in front of the Deluccis' grand abode.

'Because I'm living here now. I've got a new job, and it comes with a flat.'

Carly looks dubious, and so she should. I haven't even told Rob that we're staying here, and now I feel terrible. But what can I do? I can't possibly tell him the truth, that I'm trying to dig into Ally's death. That would break him even further.

'Come on. I want to show you around.'

Carly settles in quickly and seems enamoured by the impressive surroundings and immediately falls in love with

Minnie. Goldie is so sweet with her and has even bought her a doll to welcome her to her home. Even Rose seems charmed by the little girl, and I didn't think Rose could be charmed by anything or anyone. When I help Carly get dressed the next morning, I realise that she's outgrowing all of her clothes. Poor Rob hasn't even noticed.

'I think we need to buy you some more clothes,' I say. 'How about a little shopping trip?'

WE WALK to Putney High Street, and it's busy, thronging with people eager to shop, and traffic is backed up, as it so often is, all the way to Putney Bridge. Carly chatters away, and it's a relief that she's relaxed with me.

'Verity at school has got trainers that light up when she walks.'

'They sound really cool,' I say. 'We're going to have to get you new shoes too. Would you like some like Verity's?'

'Really? Can I?' Carly asks, jumping up and down, tugging at my arm.

I grin at her. 'Let's see if we can find some.'

She seems relaxed and happy with me. I wonder whether she really understands that her mummy will never come back. Whether the loss and sadness will creep up on her the older she gets. I feel a relief that I'm able to be there for her, to care for this little girl who is so deserving of love.

We just miss the little green man that signals we can cross the road. If I had been alone, I would have run across, but the sense of responsibility of having Carly with me weighs heavily. So we wait as the traffic whizzes past, and the crowd of pedestrians builds behind us.

A red double-decker bus is coming down the hill, and then suddenly, I feel a massive push in my back, as if someone had placed the palm of their hand in the small of my back and shoved me. I feel my feet slipping from underneath me, and in that long, horrifying second, I let go of Carly's hand. I stumble forwards, my left ankle giving way, and as the massive flash of red looms down on me, I hear the rumbling of the wheels, the collective gasping of breaths, a scream, and I ready myself for the end.

It doesn't come.

I'm on the road, my palms and knees on the tarmac. The red bus passes just millimetres from my face, the hot air and fumes choking me. A car horn reverberates in my ears. But then I feel strong hands pulling me up, voices of concern and Carly's cry. I want to sob with relief that my instinct was to let go of Carly's hand. If I had to go under the wheels of the bus, then so be it, but little Carly deserves life.

'Are you alright?' A man in a navy suit has both his arms under my armpits, and all I think is, *Why is he wearing a suit on a Saturday morning?*

'Are you hurt?' A woman with tight grey curls peers at me, her stale breath too close to my face.

'I'm fine,' I say, stepping back onto the pavement as the crowd of pedestrians surges forwards across the zebra crossing. 'Someone pushed me.' I glance around to try to spot someone who might look suspicious, someone I know perhaps. But I don't recognise any faces, and there's no one loitering, obviously watching me.

I grab Carly's hand and see the tears coursing down her cheeks. 'It's alright, sweetheart,' I say, forgetting about my sore hands and sweeping her up into my arms. 'Silly me. I tripped, but no harm done.'

'You sure you're alright?' the man in the suit asks. He must be mid-fifties with kindly eyes and dark hair that's greying at the temples.

'Thank you. I slipped. It was silly. Thank you so much.'

'In which case I'll be off.' He sprints across the road just as the pedestrian crossing stops bleeping. I shout, 'Thank you,' again, but I'm not sure that he hears me.

'We're safe, Carly,' I say, placing kisses on her cheek. This little girl doesn't deserve any more shocks. 'Let's go and get a drink, and then we'll find you a pretty new dress and those shoes that you wanted.'

'Are your hands hurt?' she asks. I hold up my palms for inspection and see some gravel has embedded in my right palm. I wipe it on a tissue.

'Nothing that won't wash off, and it doesn't hurt.'

'I think you're very brave,' Carly says with sincerity. I would like to say that it's she who is the brave one, but I just smile weakly.

As we walk slowly along the pavement, as far away from the edge of the road as possible, I can't help but relive that moment. I didn't slip. Without a shadow of doubt, I was pushed with considerable force. Whoever did it wanted me to fall into the path of that bus. Why would someone do that? And how come no one else noticed?

It isn't until many hours later, when Carly, exhausted from our extensive shopping spree, is fast asleep on the sofa in my small living room that I wonder. Was I targeted for that push, or was it random? Has someone been following me, and if so, is it because of my probing into the Deluccis? After all, I'm here under false pretences. I groan. It's not normal what I'm doing. I shouldn't be here, I shouldn't be in this household, doing a job that's within my capabilities, but which I'm not trained for. I shouldn't be suspicious of these people who have only been good to me. What I should do is accept the police investigation into Ally's death and get myself out of here. I wonder if it's not just Rob who needs help. Perhaps I do too. Perhaps the horror of Ally's death has dredged up old suppressed memories. The void that will never be filled by the premature death of our parents. The way I stepped straight into the parental role despite being so young. But one thing I do know for certain is that I can't possibly put Carly in danger, and for that reason alone, I need to get back to my ordinary life. My cosy maisonette and my bookkeeping work beckon.

15

ROSE

I hate Simone. I thought she was going to be better than Lauren, but no, she's just as sanctimonious and full of herself. How dare she try to stop me from doing what I want to do! It's like she's my mother, the way she bosses me around. It was so humiliating when she stopped me from going out with Tony the other evening. I was going to slip out the back, but Tony got fed up waiting for me, and I heard the roar of his motorbike as he sped away. I sent him a text saying I wasn't feeling well because how's it going to look if he thinks I'm subject to curfews. I'm pretty sure he thinks I'm older than I am and certainly not still at school. Not that he's ever asked me what I do during the daytime. We've met up three times so far, and it's either been late afternoon or on a Saturday, so I haven't had to lie. I could just ignore Mum and Dad, but I'm worried they'll chuck me out of the house. I mean, they probably wouldn't, but what's left for them to do? They've grounded me, taken away my money. I suppose they could send me off to boarding school, but I'd just run away, so there's little point. I can cope without money because I know how to earn it myself, but I'm not ready to leave home yet. I know that makes me sound pathetic, because there are plenty of people my age who've left home; I just don't know anyone who has. Except Mum, that is. She goes on and on about how she was self-sufficient at my age, but just because she had a shitty early life doesn't mean I have to too. So for now, I'm going to stick it out and let them think I'm playing by their rules. But I'm not, because I've got Tony.

I do need to deal with Simone, and I reckon I need to make her pay like Lauren. It was such fun nicking Mum's earrings, scarf and shoes and planting them in Lauren's room. I just regret not being there when Mum accused her of stealing. I'd have loved to have been a fly on the wall for that. But at least she got what she deserved and lost her job. But I can't pull the same trick on Simone because Mum will catch on for sure.

It was so humiliating being called in by the headmistress today. She's a stupid cow called Amber Davies, all full of herself for heading up such an important school. But let's face it, the school's only rated good because parents pay so much money to send their kids there, so they can afford the best facilities and pay for the best teachers. If I have children, I'm going to send them to the local state school. It's so wrong that money buys privilege. Anyway, Mrs Davies took off her glasses and leaned across her desk.

'What is it that you don't like about school?' she asked with her fake smile.

I didn't know where to begin, the list is so long. 'I don't find the subjects inspirational,' I said, leaning back in the chair and crossing my arms.

'It's too late to change your A-level subjects at this point, but have you decided what you're going to study at university? What fires you up, Rose?'

I felt like saying stealing, conning, pulling off the perfect crime. It would have been hysterical to see her face, but knowing her, she'd have called the police and social services, or whoever, and I'd be sent to see the school shrink and possibly locked up. No thank you.

'I'm not going to university,' I said, throwing her an earnest smile.

She paled. 'Have you discussed this with your parents?'

'It's my life, not theirs, and it's my decision.'

'So what are you going to do?'

'Join the army.'

She blinked several times because our school isn't the sort of place that has their students join up without going to university or being sponsored by a uni. I think a boy a couple of years above me got a commission and is going to be an officer. I've got no intention of joining the army because I hate everything about war, but it's hilarious watching her face.

'That's a very noble ambition,' she said eventually. 'Will you be seeking a commission?'

'God no. I want to be one of the troops. Why would I want to be an officer?'

'Well, I think this is a conversation to be had with your parents and Mrs Chambers.'

Mrs Chambers is something to do with careers advice and helping with uni applications. I've never had a conversation with her, and I don't intend to.

Anyway, I've managed to avoid any further conversations about next steps. For now, at least.

I'M AT HOME, browsing my favourite con artist website, when I get a text message from Tony. My heart skips a beat. A cliché, I know, but it really does.

Wanna meet up?

I send him a thumbs up emoji. When we were meant to be getting together the other night when stupid Simone stopped me from going out, Tony had insisted on coming to pick me up from home. I told him I was temporarily staying with my wealthy cousins. As Mum's working from home this afternoon, I suggest we meet outside the tube station.

He's already there when I arrive, leaning against his bike, looking oh-so fleek and handsome. If only some of my mates could see me now, they'd be green with envy, and I'd be the coolest girl in school.

'Hey, gorgeous. You look like you've got the weight of the world on your shoulders.'

'Just fed up. There's a woman I know who's really getting on my wick.'

He raises an eyebrow.

'I want to plant some drugs in her place. Can you get me some?' I think how hilarious it'll be if Mum finds drugs in Simone's room. 'I mean, not weed but hard stuff. Coke maybe or some pills.'

He pauses for a moment. 'Nah. You shouldn't be getting involved in shit like that. It's one thing nicking credit cards and suitcases, but drugs are the next level. You're too young.'

'I'm not that young,' I say.

'Yeah, you are. Come on. Let's go have some fun.'

It's annoying, but I'm going to have to think of another way to oust Simone.

'We're gonna do something different this afternoon,' Tony says, taking my hand. It sends a shiver right through me. 'You're Mrs Marant today, okay?'

'Sure.' *Who is Mrs Marant?* But I don't question it because, well, I just don't. Not with Tony.

We stride into some posh-looking bank that I've never

heard of, and a blonde woman steps forwards, dressed up like an air stewardess.

'How can I help you, sir, madam?' A flicker of a frown crosses her forehead. I suppose it's because Tony's holding my hand, and however much I kid myself, I know I still look young.

'We'd like to take out some cash, please,' Tony says.

'Of course, sir.' She leads us over to a counter where a man with peroxide hair smiles flirtatiously with Tony. His hairstyle is so last century.

'Good afternoon. My name is Tony. How can I help you?'

I think it's hilarious that he's called Tony too and almost burst out laughing, but my Tony gives my hand a tight squeeze.

'We'd like to take out ten thousand pounds from our joint bank account,' Tony says. He removes a chequebook from his pocket and writes out a cheque for cash for ten grand. I try not to let my eyes pop out of my head. Besides, I thought chequebooks were twentieth century and not used today.

'Have you ordered the money, Mr Marant?' the other Tony asks.

'I have indeed. I rang yesterday.'

'Fantastic. If I could have your card, please.'

My Tony hands it over, and Tony two disappears with the chequebook and card.

'A shit load of cash,' I whisper into Tony's ear.

'Shush,' he whispers back and then runs his hand down my cheek as if we're some newly-weds out on a fancy shopping trip. How I wish this weren't play acting.

A few minutes later, Tony two comes back with a large envelope.

'Could you pop your pin in the card reader, please, Mr Marant?'

I don't know how Tony knows the correct pin, but he does.

'What denomination of notes would you like, Mr Marant?'

'In fifties, please.'

A few moments later, Tony two is counting out two hundred fifty-pound notes. It's a lot, but somehow, I thought ten grand would look more impressive than that. And then it's popped into a large envelope and handed across the counter.

When we're outside the bank, I do a little dance around Tony. 'How did you pull that one off?' I ask.

'Sometimes a partner is best off knowing as little as possible,' he says enigmatically. 'Let's go shopping. What would you like?'

'You mean proper shopping, jewellery?'

'If you want.'

'I'd like some more huggie earrings and a diamond stud for my belly button piercing.'

'I think we can manage that,' he says with a grin. But he's dropped my hand now, and when we go into the shops, it's like his mind is on other things, and he's really not that bothered with me. Nevertheless, it's a great afternoon, and just because I can, I nick an expensive ring and give it to Tony as a thank you. Because that's what partners do, isn't it?

THE NEXT MORNING, Simone is out with Carly. She's cute, that kid, just a shame she's got such a cow as an aunt. Anyway, I take a couple of half-drunk bottles of vodka and gin from Dad's drinks cabinet, pour the contents into empty water bottles (because it's not like I'm going to tip them down the drain) and hurry downstairs to Simone's flat. I hide one bottle under her bed and another in her wardrobe, and then I decide that a half-drunk bottle would be good to have too, so I nip back upstairs, take a bottle of brandy – one that looks expensive and hopefully Dad will miss – and stick that in her wardrobe too. Yay! Now I just have to drop the hint to my parents that I smell booze on her breath. Byee, Simone!

16

GOLDIE

I thought the evening at the art gallery went well. The paintings were hideous. Who would want splodges of blacks and greys on their walls? So depressing, and despite staring at them for a long time, I couldn't see the hidden meaning. Perhaps I'm just lacking in aesthetic understanding, but they weren't for me. There were lots of wealthy people, who not only were buying the ghastly art but also seemed genuinely interested in our new film project. I gave out business cards to at least ten people, many of whom were fascinated by the theme of the next film. *What She Knew* is another psychological thriller, but it's set in the world of art, about a professor, his student who becomes his wife, and their best friends who run a London auction house. Obviously, those art enthusiasts were gushing about the film, but words are cheap. Now I need to find out whether any of them will put their money into the project.

I'm methodically calling them up, but in each conversation I'm met with resistance. *It's a great project but not what we're looking for at the moment. Our next investors meeting isn't for another quarter. Leave it with us, and we'll get back to you.* I'm really struggling, and if we don't get more funds in soon, the whole project will be in jeopardy.

At least I'm having lunch with my friend Jana.

JANA ALSO HAS her own production company, but she produces documentary films that get sold to the likes of National Geographic and the BBC. She's been a kind of mentor to me; about a decade older, there's nothing about this industry or the people in it she doesn't know. We're both so busy, we don't meet up as often as we should, so it's a rare treat to be having a couple of hours with her.

The restaurant is in Soho, a new Italian restaurant that has been getting rave reviews. There is green foliage every-where. To the left of the entrance is a verdant living wall, and hanging plants extend their tendrils over the centre of each glass table. The place has the look and the humidity of a greenhouse, and to me it screams the tropics rather than Italy. Jana is sitting at a table by the window, and she waves at me as I enter.

'Hello, darling,' she greets me in her typically exuberant style, with a kiss on each cheek followed by one extra. 'It's three kisses in Europe,' she once told me, although why she's affected the European way of greeting, I'm not quite sure, because Jana is South African, and despite living in the UK for the past three decades, she's never lost her accent.

'You look well,' I say as I settle into my chair, noticing her sleek grey bob and the beautifully cut all-black outfit that is her signature look. The only colour Jana wears is around her neck, and today she's sporting a necklace of chunky turquoise beads.

'And you look beautiful but exhausted,' she replies.

I sigh. I don't think I'm beautiful, but I'm certainly exhausted.

'What's been happening?' she asks as she pours me a glass of sparkling water and a white wine, which I haven't asked for.

'We're finishing off *The Insomniac*, and I'm trying to raise funds and get everything lined up for the filming of *What She Knew*, our next film in the pipeline.'

'We'll talk about that in a moment, but how's the family?'

'Good,' I say, although I can hardly tell Jana the truth, that Rose is out of control, Florian is shrinking inside himself daily, and Braun, well, we're both so busy on different projects, we barely see each other. Being in the same industry, Jana and I only gloss the surface of our personal lives and never really share confidences. In some ways that's a shame because I'm sure she would be very understanding, but we work in a small world, and although I doubt she'd let slip any gossip, I can't take the risk. I have no doubt she feels the same way. 'We have a new family help. She's super organised, and it's such a relief having her around.'

'How about you?'

But Jana doesn't get the chance to answer my question because a waiter comes to take our order. After taking a quick glance at the menu, I order sea bream. Jana goes for a chicken dish.

'And how are you finding it, raising funds for your next film?' she asks.

'Really tough. Much harder than the previous two times, which doesn't make any sense to me. We have a track record now.'

'Mmm,' Jana says, taking a large sip of wine.

'What aren't you telling me?' I lean forwards, putting my elbows on the table.

'The rumours,' Janna says. 'People have heard about the fatality.'

'But that was nothing to do with us!' I exclaim. 'It was just a tragedy that happened after filming.'

'Yes, yes, I know.' Janna waves her hand around. 'But people talk. The girl was found with drugs in her system, wasn't she?'

I have to nod reluctantly.

'And there's talk that drugs were rife on set.'

'But that's not true!' I say. *What nonsense and speculation.* 'Who's spreading these rumours?'

'I don't know, Goldie, but that's what's being said. And unfortunately perception is reality.'

'You think that's why I'm not getting the funding?'

She shrugs her shoulders. 'You know what this industry is like. The slightest whiff of anything unsavoury and people run for the hills.'

'But it's not true.'

'So you're going to have to address the issue head-on. It's best you know what people are saying, isn't it?'

Jana is right, and although I have to strenuously deny it, I'm beginning to wonder if there might be some truth in these rumours. I wouldn't have thought that Ally was the type of girl to be on drugs, but that is undisputed thanks to the autopsy. Perhaps Braun let things slip on set. He's not going to like me questioning him, but for the future of our business, that's what I'm going to have to do. I'm also going to need to chase the PR company and find out what they're doing to mitigate these rumours.

I change the conversation, and the rest of the meal is spent amiably, discussing Jana's plans, her family and the exotic holidays she manages to add on to her times spent visiting her crew on locations.

It's been a tonic seeing my friend, and as I get into my taxi, I feel much better. At least now I know why we're not getting the funding. She's right, knowledge is power. But that positivity doesn't last long. I get a phone call from America.

'I'm sorry, but Brendan is withdrawing from being considered for the leading role in *What She Knew*,' his agent says in a languishing drawl, which suggests she's not sorry at all but is probably delighted because Brendan has been tempted with a much more lucrative role in a fancier location, and his agent is counting the dollars that will be pouring into her bank account.

'That's very disappointing. Is there anything we can do to persuade him to change his mind? He's perfect for the leading role.'

'Sorry, darling. It's a no can do from us. Best of luck with the film.' And then she cuts the call.

I slam my hand on the back seat, eliciting a look of concern from the cabbie. It feels like everything is going against us for this new film. My head pounds with the beginnings of a migraine, and frankly, all I feel like doing is going to bed and hiding under the duvet for the next few weeks.

BACK AT HOME, I take a deep breath, cuddle Minnie and stride into the kitchen, where Simone is leaning into the oven.

'Something smells good,' I say. Little Carly is sitting at the kitchen table, colouring vigorously. She's such a sweet child.

'I've made a carrot cake for you, as I know that chocolate isn't any good for your migraines. And there's lasagne for supper. I know you didn't ask me to cook, but I have the time.'

'Oh, Simone.' I have to blink to stop my eyes from welling up. This woman really is a godsend. She's probably going out of her way to do nice things for me because I've let her have her niece to stay. All I can think of is thank goodness for Simone.

'I'm going to check up on Florian, and I want you to sign

off early today. Go and have a lovely time with Carly. In fact, why don't you take her out for a pizza or something.' I remove my wallet from my bag and produce a couple of twenty-pound notes, which I hold out to Simone.

'Oh no, I couldn't possibly,' she says. For someone who is normally so together, it seems as if she's wrong-footed some-how. I wonder for a moment if I've offended her. 'That's really kind of you, but you pay me enough. And yes, I will take Carly out for a meal.' She turns to the little girl. 'Would you like to go to Pizza Please for supper?'

Carly jumps up.

'Please take the money,' I say. Simone accepts the cash, but reluctantly.

BRAUN IS home in time for supper. He comes up behind me and kisses my neck.

'We need to talk,' I say quietly.

'What about?'

'There's a rumour going around that there was a drug problem on the set of *The Insomniac*.'

'What the hell!' Braun explodes. He does that sometimes. I used to find his unpredictability exciting. Not so much these days.

But then Florian walks into the kitchen.

'Later,' I murmur to Braun.

I try to ignore the fact that he sinks two glasses of wine straight down, and when the four of us are sitting at the table, he puts on this weird and false bravado. Something is very amiss.

'So, kiddos, how's school?' Braun asks.

'Mrs Davies wanted to see me yesterday,' Rose says.

'Oh yeah.' Braun probably doesn't even know who she is,

but then he's never really been interested in the children's education.

'Why did the headteacher want to see you?' I ask, for my husband's benefit and because I'm worried. I had hoped that Rose's lack of application to her schoolwork had been addressed. Both Simone and I have had words with her, and I assumed everything had been resolved.

'She wanted to know what I'm going to do when I leave school. Which universities I'm applying to.'

'Have you decided?' I ask, feeling hopeful for a second. Rose has avoided the conversation up until now, yet I'm aware that's another thing on my never-ending list. Rose will have to get her university applications in within the next few weeks, and I've no doubt she'll need my help.

'Yes. I'm not going to uni. I'm joining the army.'

Braun drops his knife, which clatters onto the plate. 'You're what?'

'I thought I'd do my bit for the country and sign up. You've all been telling me I need more discipline in my life.'

'Are you sure, Rose?' I ask as dismay sinks down onto my shoulders. Rose is artistic, quirky, non-conformist. I just can't see her in the army. And then there's that awful shadow of what if there's a war; will my daughter have to fight?

'I think that's cool,' Florian says.

'Thought you would.' She grins.

Braun and I look at each other, anxiety reflected in both of our faces. For the first time in ages, my husband is lost for words.

'Aren't you going to congratulate me for making such a brave decision, for doing what is right?'

'Are you aware of what is required?' I ask.

'I suppose you could make an officer,' Braun says.

'I'm not going to be an officer. I want to be part of the troops not some stuck-up boss girl who tells everyone else what to do. Just because Mum is a boss doesn't mean I have to be one too. I mean, it's not like it's making her happy, is it?' What does she mean by that? Rose takes a large swig of water and then grins at me, her teeth biting her lower lip. 'Anyway, we've got more pressing problems as a family.'

'What do you mean?' I ask. I'm going to need to take some more migraine medication.

'I think Simone's a drinker.'

'A drinker?' I ask.

'I smelled alcohol on her breath when she did the school run this afternoon. I mean, it's pretty crap, isn't it? She had Carly in the car with us too. It's one thing putting me and Florian at risk, but her niece as well. It must mean she's got a mega problem.'

'Have you ever smelled booze on her?' Braun asks me.

'No.' And I haven't. I wonder if this is one of Rose's ruses.

'I think you should check out her room. I bet she's got a secret stash of wine, or perhaps she's just nicking yours, Dad.'

Florian sniggers.

I feel sick.

'God, I hope she's not like Lauren,' I say.

It isn't until the middle of the night, by which time Braun is snoring heavily, that I remember we never finished our conversation about the drugs on set.

17

SIMONE

I didn't mean to overhear their conversation.

After taking Carly out for an early supper at Pizza Please, it was difficult to get her to settle. I don't suppose the mountain of ice cream with a bucketload of sweeties on top have helped. But Carly couldn't sleep. I tried everything to settle her: bedtime stories, stroking her hair, singing, but then she said she wanted a hot chocolate because Mummy used to give her that. I had milk in my little fridge but not cocoa powder. I knew Goldie wouldn't mind me taking a spoonful or two, so I went upstairs. I was about to walk into the kitchen when I heard Rose say my name. We're programmed to listen out for our names, and of course I came to a silent full stop, wanting to hear what she was saying. Can you imagine my shock when I heard her say that she thinks I'm a drinker, that I have bottles of booze hidden in my room? I felt like storming in there and grabbing the girl, telling her she's a liar and a troublemaker. But what shocked me even more was neither Goldie nor Braun doubted what Rose said. How can they not realise that their troubled daughter is a liar, a sensationalist desperate for attention, and she'll say anything to get a reaction or to stir up trouble? And then Goldie says, 'I hope she's not like Lauren.' What does she mean by that?

I say nothing. Instead, I turn around and tiptoe back down the stairs. I can see exactly what's happening here. Rose is gunning for me, doing her best to get me fired because I've been cramping her style. Of course she doesn't like me stopping her from going out, or telling her off, or talking to her parents about her, but it's not Rose who is my employer. My loyalty lies with Goldie, and I have a duty of care towards Rose. To stop her behaving like an idiot and ruining her life.

At the bottom of the stairs I stop still. I can't believe I'm taking this so seriously, thinking my loyalty lies with Goldie. Of course it doesn't. I keep on forgetting that this isn't a real job; I'm here for a purpose and a purpose I had better let go of before things really get out of hand. I'm just too diligent.

Sighing, I walk into the small living room, wondering how I can persuade Carly to have hot milk without cocoa, but I don't have to worry. She's fast asleep, breathing deeply and clutching her teddy.

I pour myself a glass of red wine, and no, I'm not much of a drinker. It's rare that I drink alcohol by myself, but tonight I really feel like I need it. I wonder if Rose had anything to do with Lauren leaving this job. If she's spreading false rumours about me, the chances are she might have done the same to my predecessor. There's only one way to find out. I send Lauren a text and ask if she's got time for a chat.

I turn my laptop on and browse Netflix, but it's hard to concentrate. There I was, convinced I needed to leave this job, but now I don't want to. I know Rose is only a kid, but she's accused me of something I haven't done, and that somehow, in a minor way, mirrors my feelings about what happened to Ally. My sister was accused of drug taking and stealing a car, yet I'm sure she was also innocent. It's made me feel like I should keep probing, keep investigating. I'm damned if I'm going to be accused of something I haven't done. But I know that I need to be doubly careful, if only for Carly's sake. The more I think about that hand on my back on the edge of the road, the more I realise it must have been random. Unless, of course, it's Rose. There's only one thing for it. I'm going to have to confront her.

About an hour later, Lauren calls me. I take the phone into the bedroom and shut the door.

'How are things?' she asks.

'Yeah, fine. This is a weird question, and I hope you don't mind me asking. But what was your relationship like with Rose?'

There's a heavy beat of silence. 'Not good. She loathed me.'

'Because you told her off and brought all her misde-meanours to her parents' attention?' I suggest.

'Exactly. She's just a wayward kid.'

'Did she accuse you of something?'

Lauren sighs. 'Yes.'

'And she got you fired?'

'Has the same thing happened to you?'

'Not yet, but I overheard her telling Goldie that I'm an alcoholic and I drove the kids to school under the influence.'

'Why doesn't that surprise me?' Lauren says. 'She set me up. Nicked some of her mother's belongings and stashed them in my room. Goldie found them and fired me.'

'I'm so sorry, Lauren. Didn't you try to explain?'

'Of course, but Goldie was never going to believe me over her precious daughter. I knew there was nothing I could do to prove I hadn't stolen the items, so I just left. I didn't like the job much anyway.'

'Still, that's a horrible thing to have happened to you. I'm sorry.'

'What are you going to do about the accusations made against you?'

'Confront Rose.'

'Good luck with that,' Lauren says.

BEFORE GOING TO SLEEP, I search my rooms, and unsurprisingly I find two empty bottles of vodka and a half-full bottle of expensive-looking brandy. There's not much I can do about them now, so I put them in a carrier bag, double-check on Carly and go to sleep.

The next morning, Goldie takes the kids to school, and Braun leaves at the same time. I suppose Goldie's worried that I might really be under the influence. But it gives me the opportunity to drop Carly off at nursery school and to dispose of the bottles. It's a waste, I know, but I pour the brandy down the drain, and I take the empty bottles to the bottle bank outside Sainsbury's supermarket. And then I head back to the house to go through Goldie's emails and correspondence.

No one is at home, but as I'm walking through the hallway, I see Braun's briefcase propped up on the bench. He must have forgotten it. I hesitate, but not for long. I whip the briefcase away and take it upstairs and onto the landing, where the tall window looks out onto the driveway, so I'll see if either Goldie or Braun come home. And then I open the case and take out the papers. There's a script, a letter from the studio and a sheaf of bank statements. But these aren't statements for the account in Goldie and Braun's joint names, because I have access to that account to pay their household bills. And it's not for Delucci Productions, which I assume Goldie oversees. This is an account in Braun's name only, and the figures are shocking. He is massively overdrawn, by tens of thousands of pounds. What a shock! It's not even clear what he's been spending the money on, but large sums are going out to names of people and businesses that mean nothing to me, and nothing is coming in. I wonder if Delucci Productions is also in financial trouble. I'm sure that there will be statements in Goldie's study, but she keeps her filing unit there locked. And then I hear the crunch of tires on the gravel drive, and I shove the papers back into the briefcase, hurry downstairs and drop the case on the bench before turning down the hallway to the kitchen just as the front door opens.

I turn around. It's Goldie. I wonder whether I should tell her that I overheard what Rose said, but from the harried look on her face, I decide not to. It will be better to confront Rose directly. For the rest of the day, I do the job that I'm employed to do. Goldie goes out again; I collect Carly from nursery and, later, Florian from school. A little after 5 pm, Rose comes into the house. Leaving Carly at the kitchen table doing some colouring, I hurry upstairs after Rose and knock on her door. She doesn't answer, so I swing it open.

She swivels around, her hands on her hips. 'I didn't say that you could come in.'

'I don't need your permission. I know what you've been up to, Rose.'

The girl pales and takes a step backwards, clutching a chair.

'I rarely drink. I am not an alcoholic or a thief. And if you ever mess with me again, you will be very, very sorry.'

Rose's mouth drops open.

'Do you understand what I'm saying?'

She nods at me, her eyes large and startled. She looks very young, and I realise that, most likely, no one in authority has ever really stood up to her. I suppose she knows that her parents will never chuck her out of the house, that she will always have a roof over her head and the unconditional love of her family. But she doesn't know me at all. I've shocked her, and that feels good. I turn on my heel and stride out of her room.

18

ROSE

'Rose!'

Mum storms into my room, her hands on her hips, her eyes flashing with anger and the little blue vein in her right temple pulsating like it always does when she's angry. What is it this time? I brace myself.

'I've checked Simone's rooms, and there are no bottles of alcohol there. In fact, I don't think I've even seen Simone with a glass of wine. Why did you say that about her?'

Mum narrows her eyes at me. The look doesn't suit her.

'Answer me, Rose!'

'I dunno.' But I do know, and I'm livid. How come Simone got rid of the bottles? Did she listen to our conversation at the dinner table, or is she one of those neat freaks who clears out her cupboards every night because she's got nothing better to do?

'You must not go around spreading gossip. It's wicked, and it could potentially lose people their jobs, saying things like that.'

'That's me all over, isn't it, Mum? Wicked, evil, the bitch of a daughter.'

'I didn't say that.' Mum looks contrite now. 'It's horrible behaviour spreading malicious gossip. It's just as well I checked and didn't say anything to Simone.'

'Yeah, well.'

'You could at least say sorry,' Mum says.

'Sorry,' I mumble.

That must be good enough because Mum sighs and leaves the room.

I'm so pissed off that the ruse didn't work. I'm going to have to come up with something else, and for someone who is never short of ideas, I'm out of them right now. I need to see Tony. He's bound to have some suggestions.

That's the thing I like about Tony. There are no games. He replies straight away. If he's busy, he tells me; if not, we arrange to meet. I know where I stand with him, and he makes me feel great about myself, as if my opinions matter, as if I'm an adult, even an equal. It's not like that at home or at school, where I'm treated like a kid. And I'm not a kid. Even though he made it clear we're partners and he doesn't want a relationship, I can tell that he likes me. Perhaps he's got a girl-friend and doesn't feel he can ditch her. I've never asked. One day I'll pluck up the courage and ask him more about himself. I can see me and Tony together. Yes, he's probably a bit old for me, but that's just a societal convention. Next year I'll be eighteen, and then I can get together with whomever I want. Probably could now, but it's really not cool that I'm still at school. I'd rather make my move on Tony when I've left and am out in the real world. And no, I've no intention of joining the army. I just wanted to see Mum and Dad's reac-tion. Can you imagine me in the army? I'd tell the sergeant major or whatever he's called to f off within the first five minutes. No, my talents lie elsewhere. I'm thinking I might get into bitcoins or something more edgy perhaps, on the fringes of society. Another thing I can ask Tony's advice on.

I send him a WhatsApp message.

You free?

He replies immediately.

For u, yes.

Can you pick me up from the bottom of the road?

Sure. Be there in an hour. X

OMG – he put an X after his message. I overheard Flora talking in the canteen at school. She's one of the pretty, cool girls, the queen-bee type and a complete bitch. But she said when a boy puts an X at the end of a message, that actually means something. It's not like us girls who chuck them out without thinking about it. My stomach is full of butterflies, and I've got an hour to get myself ready.

I put on eyeliner and red lipstick. It's the first time I've worn it since I nicked it a couple of weeks back, and I'm not totally sure about the colour. It makes my lips look huge, but that's a good thing, isn't it? I wear a boob tube under my biker jacket. It shows off my curves and my flat stomach, and I pair it with skinny jeans. I'll probably be cold because it's quite bitter out there, but Tony will keep me warm. I stare at myself in the mirror. It's biker girl chic, and with the make-up I look at least ten years older, which is a good thing.

I tiptoe out of the house because the last thing I need is for the bitch Simone to see me or for Mum to ask what the hell I'm wearing on a winter's day. Tony isn't there when I get to the bottom of the road, which isn't like him because he's normally early. But I'm okay to wait. I drape myself over a bollard, making my tits stick out a bit more, with my legs casually crossed. I'm beginning to wonder whether I've been stood up when the roar of a bike gets louder. And there he is, pulling up beside me.

'Hop on, then,' he says, handing me the spare helmet.

'Where are we going?' I ask.

'Thought we'd stop for a coffee and then decide.'

That sounds good to me.

ABOUT TWENTY MINUTES LATER, we're in some industrial estate where I've never been before, the back of Vauxhall by the looks of things. Tony leads me into a cafe, well, more of a greasy spoon than a coffee shop and certainly nowhere I'd want to go by myself. There's a woman wearing a pink pinafore pouring coffee from a jug, and she reminds me of some brassy woman from a film about an American diner, other than she's not American. She's pure cockney.

'Hiya, Tones,' she says, blowing him a kiss. I have a surprising twinge of jealousy in my stomach, which is stupid because I can't imagine Tony going for an old woman like her. 'Your regular?'

'Yes, please, Annie.'

'And what will the young lady have?'

'A black coffee, please.' I don't really want a black coffee. I don't like the taste, but it wouldn't look cool if I asked for a Coke.

'So how are things?' Tony asks, leaning across the plastic table, staring me in the eyes as if he really cares.

'There's this woman who works for my family, and she's a total bitch. I want to make her pay. Any bright ideas?'

'Mm,' he says, leaning back in his chair so that his abs show through his black T-shirt. 'Just her or your family too?'

'The lot of them. I'm leaving home soon.' And then I pinch myself because I told him I was living with my wealthy cousins.

'No lies with me, partner,' he says, winking at me. 'That fancy house is yours, isn't it, and it's your parents who are giving you grief?'

I feel my cheeks redden and nod reluctantly because it makes me look like a kid bitching about my parents. Too late now.

Tony rubs his chin. 'You could always make them pay?'

'How? With money?'

'Nah. Money doesn't always work with family. You need to teach them a lesson.' He thinks for a moment, his blue eyes staring up at the ceiling. 'Perhaps you could disappear for a couple of days, and then they'd be really stressed about you.'

I shuffle forwards, a buzz of excitement in my stomach. 'You mean kidnap me or something?'

'Could do,' he says nonchalantly as if this were a perfectly ordinary conversation.

'That's a great idea.'

'Get them really worried about you, because I assume they still love you, even though you don't get on from time to time? I mean, they haven't chucked you out of the house or disinherited you or anything, have they?'

'No, I suppose they do care.' In fact, I know that's true. Mum and Dad let me get away with loads of stuff, really.

'We could get them to pay a ransom and split the money.'

I think about that for a moment. 'But the money is mine anyway because I'm going to inherit it all. Me and my younger brother.'

'Good point. How about me taking twenty-five percent because I'm the one taking the risk by kidnapping you, and you'll get the rest.'

I can't stop smiling. This is such a good idea. Tony is a

star. Mum and Dad are going to be so worried about me, and of course they'll pay out. Then I'll have loads of money, so I can start my new life as soon as my A levels are over, or perhaps I'll leave school sooner, as it's not like my A levels are going to help me get on in life. Experience is way more important. I can just see myself in a studio apartment perhaps in a warehouse somewhere, one of those trendy places with brick walls and high ceilings and exposed pipes. I'll get a bank of computer screens and learn about cryptocurrency and go to MeetUps and hang out with all the nerdy types. And if I have money left over, I'll give it to Joe and the other homeless people like him who are treated like total shit by our heartless society.

'It sounds like a brilliant idea,' I say. 'And such fun.'

We grin at each other.

'Right then. How are we going to make it happen?' Tony asks.

19

SIMONE

Goldie has gone away for a couple of days, and I have a long list of instructions as to what I have to do in her absence. The number one priority is getting Florian to the coach, ready for his school trip, and I'm checking off the list provided by his teacher.

'Where are your shorts?' I ask Florian, who is dawdling in his en suite bathroom, supposedly packing his washbag, but he's been in there a long time.

'Dunno,' he says through the open door. I walk over to look at him. He's sitting on the closed toilet lid, his chin resting in his hands. He looks like he has the weight of the world on him.

'What's up, Florian?'

He looks at me with big eyes. 'I don't want to go.'

'I know you don't. And frankly, I don't blame you. I wouldn't want to do an outdoor course in the rain and the wind, but, you know, the things we least want to do often turn out to be the most fun.'

'It won't be.'

'You don't know that, do you?'

He sniffs.

'I told Mum I didn't want to go, but she said I had to. It's not fair.'

'You'll have fun camping with your friends.'

He goes very still and does that thing with his shoulders as if he's shrinking in on himself.

'You have friends, don't you?' I ask, crouching down in front of him.

He won't meet my eyes, but he shakes his head.

'Oh, sweetie, I'm sure there are some boys you like.'

'No one likes me,' he mutters. 'They all pick on me because I'm thick and I'm small and I'm rubbish at sport.'

'Are they being horrible to you?'

Florian's nod is barely perceptible.

'Have you told anyone at school or your mum?'

He shakes his head this time.

'Oh, sweetie, that's miserable. Do you want me to say something to the teacher when I drop you off?'

He looks up at me with a startled expression. 'No, it'll only make it worse. Can't I just stay at home? Mum's away, so she doesn't even need to know, and I'll stay with you and play with Carly.'

I squeeze his shoulder. 'As much as I'd like to have you here, you're going to have to go. It's what your parents want, and I'm sure it'll be so much more fun than you anticipate.' I don't believe that for one second, but what can I do? Goldie has gone to Milan. She'll be on a flight right now and then in meetings all day. She told me she'd be out of contact, and in case of an emergency, I should contact her husband. I can't imagine Braun showing much sympathy for Florian's plight, but I'll try calling him anyway.

'Why don't you finish packing, and I'll call your dad and see what he says?'

'Okay.'

Braun doesn't answer his phone. I try again five minutes later, and again when we're in the car, and for the final time when we pull up in front of the school. I get that he's busy doing whatever he does with his film, but wouldn't he check his phone sometime? And shouldn't he have an iota of concern that I'm calling him when he knows that I'm looking after his children and Goldie is in an airplane. I hold Carly's hand as we accompany Florian to the coach. His head is bowed, and he doesn't once glance up or acknowledge any of the other excited youngsters. I hand his bag to the coach driver, who is tossing the kids' belongings into the belly of the bus.

'I'm sorry,' I whisper to him. It feels like I'm releasing him into the lions' den, full of confident, physically bigger children than him, and I just pray that the trip isn't as dreadful as Florian expects. I wonder if I should say something to the teacher who's ticking the kids off as they get onto the bus. She looks cheerful, if a little too eager and sporty. But I don't. With his shoulders hunched, Florian walks up the steps of the bus. I watch as he makes his way along the aisle of the coach, taking a window seat near the middle of the bus. I wave at him, and he gives me a weak smile in return, and I wait there until all the children are seated and the coach starts up with a cough and a splutter, then I give him a thumbs up and mouth *good luck*. And I still wait until the bus has disappeared around the corner.

Poor Florian.

'What are we standing here for?' Carly asks, tugging me out of my concern for the Deluccis' son.

As I'm driving home after dropping Carly at nursery, I wonder whether Ally was feeling bullied on the film set. Is that why she felt she had to resort to taking drugs? But no.

Surely she would have said something to Rob or me. Ally was a grown woman with resilience. She had to have resilience because she'd faced rejection so many times before striking gold with the Deluccis. If it had been me, I would have given up years before. It was a wonder how she could go to audition after audition, be told no, your face doesn't fit or you're too stiff or you're too old or you're too young, or worse still, hear nothing at all, yet she still picked herself up and went back for more. Ally was strong, and she wasn't a victim. I recap what I know, which is still so little. She left the set with Braun, so the question now is, was he with her in Goldie's car? The police said she was alone, but was she really? Could Braun have asked her to drive him home?

I also know that Braun is broke and owes serious money to the bank. Yet I'm not sure how that knowledge makes any difference to my investigation into what happened to Ally. It's not like she or Rob had any money, so she couldn't have loaned anything to him. And for all I know, Goldie might be perfectly aware of Braun's financial predicament.

When I'm back at their house, I check that no one else is home and decide to have another snoop. This time I go up to Braun's dressing room. It's smaller than Goldie's, a square space lined with walnut wood cupboards and drawers, a room I go into regularly to put his clothes away when they return from the dry cleaners, beautifully ironed and smelling faintly of chemicals. But I've never snuck a look into his drawers or searched through his pockets. I lift three jackets and several pairs of trousers off the rail and take them into the bedroom, laying them on the bed. I put my hand in the pockets of the jackets, but all three are empty. I'm now feeling inside the pockets of the trousers.

'Hello!'

I jump. Quite literally, and drop the trousers I'm holding. Braun is walking towards me, a broad smile on his face.

'It would be better if you felt inside my pockets when I'm wearing them,' he says. 'You might find a nice surprise.' He walks right up to me, his eyes fixed on mine, his lips slightly apart, and takes my hand. He then places it on his groin.

I recoil immediately, harshly pulling my hand away from him. 'What are you doing?' I ask in disgust.

'Oh come on, Simone. I've seen the way you look at me. I had three missed calls from you this morning. Let's not beat around the bush. Goldie is away, and you want it as much as I do.'

I feel sick. This man is coming onto me, and he's not even being subtle about it. We're standing here in his marital bedroom, and he disgusts me. He's picked on the wrong person.

'You have got it totally wrong, Braun. You are my employer, and whilst I respect you, I don't find you attractive and have no desire to have any kind of relationship.'

'Who said anything about a relationship?' he asks, running his tongue along his flabby lips.

'You're married, Braun. This is horrible, immoral.'

'So what is the truth, Miss Goody-two-shoes? I know all about you. That you're in this job under false pretences. You thought that neither Goldie nor I would follow up on the so-called references on your CV, but you're wrong. I know they were made up, blatant lies. You're the one with the dubious morals around here, Simone. Surely you know it's a terrible mistake to bite the hand that feeds you.'

'What are you saying?' My voice comes out in a hoarse whisper.

'That I always get what I want. I know you're attracted to me, most women are, but you're in denial.'

'That's not true.' And then terrified that he's going to attack me, I turn on my heel and flee the room, leaving his clothes lying on the bed, running down the stairs so fast I almost slip. I race into the kitchen, through the utility room and downstairs to my basement flat, locking the door behind me. Leaving the key in the lock so he can't get in with a spare key, I wonder if he's going to come after me. I race to the external door and bolt it from the inside, then I wait, my heart pounding, a sickness in my stomach, but I don't hear any footsteps. I've been living in the same house as him, and I had no idea how awful he was. What a horrible brute of a man.

I sink onto my bed before getting up again and pulling the chest of drawers across the door for good measure. I don't believe Braun would actually hurt me; he's probably just so used to pretty actresses fawning at his feet, doing whatever it takes to get roles in his films. It's such a cliché, and it sickens me. I don't suppose anyone has actually rejected him. I feel so sorry for Goldie being married to such a revolting man. And then with a heavy heart, I wonder, did he behave like that towards Ally? I just pray he didn't force Ally to do anything she didn't want because that would be too much to bear.

After a few minutes of hearing nothing, I realise I can't hide down here for long. I've got things to do in the house, not least go through Goldie's emails, collect Carly from nursery and prepare food for Braun and Rose's supper, but now I'm scared. I don't want to be alone with this man. Surely he wouldn't really try to do something?

As I pace up and down the small room, I make a decision. I'm handing in my notice as soon as Goldie returns. This job just isn't worth it. I've found out nothing concrete, and all I'm getting is hassle and headaches. Enough is enough.

20

ROSE

I can barely contain my excitement. Tonight is the night. Tonight I'm going to be 'kidnapped' by Tony, and my parents and Simone will be in a complete panic. I wonder whether they'll call the police, whether my disappearance will make the headlines. I'll be famous, which is both a good and bad thing, because most of my scams are dependent on me being invisible. I've never been one of those people who wants fame for the sake of it. But if we get loads of money, then it'll be worth it.

It's the perfect evening because Dad announces he's going out, Mum is away, and Simone will be in her flat, looking after Carly. Even Florian is out of the house too, which is important, because it's not fair that he gets traumatised. He's troubled enough as it is.

I'm settling down for an evening in front of the telly in the living room. I never normally watch it because, firstly, I don't want to be around Mum and Dad, and secondly, YouTube is so much better. But it's easiest if I'm downstairs for when the big event happens. I'm scrolling through the channels when Simone comes bustling in, looking totally harassed.

'Your mum has asked me to pick her up from the airport.'

'What? I thought she was coming back tomorrow?'

'No, it was always today, and she should have been back by now, but her flight got delayed. She's asked if I can collect her from Heathrow.'

I can't believe I got the date wrong. I was sure she was gone for another twenty-four hours, not that it really matters because now Simone will be out of the house too, so that's good news.

'Can you babysit Carly for a couple of hours?'

'What?' It takes a moment to digest what Simone is asking. Under normal circumstances I wouldn't mind a bit because Carly's a cute kid, and perhaps Simone might even pay me for it, but I'm being kidnapped in an hour's time, and I can't have Carly around for that. 'It's really not convenient, Simone,' I say. 'Can't you ask Dad?'

'Your dad isn't answering his phone and no doubt is out having a meeting or something.'

Probably at the pub getting pissed.

'Come on, Rose. Let's not have an argument over this. Your mum has asked me to pick her up from the airport, which is a reasonable request. Carly is already in her pyjamas, so you're not required to do anything except read her a bedtime story. It's not even the end of the world if she won't go to sleep because it's Saturday tomorrow. She can snuggle up on the sofa here, and I'll put her to bed when we're back.'

What I hadn't realised was that Carly had sneaked up the stairs behind Simone and was standing there looking all cute in her pink pyjamas, clutching a toy rabbit and a blanket. It's not like I can say no in front of the kid, is it? As always, Mum and Simone have screwed things up for me. I'll have to call Tony and postpone our plans for tonight.

I purse my lips and let out a stream of air. 'Come and sit

here,' I say to Carly, patting the sofa next to me. 'Let's find something to watch on the Disney channel.'

Carly races towards me, curls her feet up underneath herself and snuggles into my side. Damn this kid. She's too adorable.

'Thanks, Rose,' Simone says. 'Be a good girl for Rose, sweetheart, and I'll see you a bit later.'

We wait for Simone to leave, and then I turn to Carly. 'What's your favourite film, or do you want to see something new?'

'Can we watch *Frozen*?' she asks with big eyes. She then sticks her thumb in her mouth, and I don't know if that's allowed or not, so I just let her.

'Sure. I'll find it.'

I turn on the film and then say to Carly, 'I'm going into the hallway to make a phone call, but just shout if you need me, alright?'

Carly nods, but she's already engrossed in *Frozen*.

I TELEPHONE TONY, but he doesn't answer, and after a few rings, the phone goes to voicemail. 'Leave a message and I'll get back to you. Or I won't.'

I don't leave a message. I send him a WhatsApp because that's where he normally responds the quickest.

Need to postpone plans for tonight. Call me.

I wait five minutes or so, but it's impossible to concentrate on the movie. Tony doesn't call. This isn't like him at all. Normally he responds quickly. I try ringing him again, but this time it goes straight to voicemail, suggesting he's got the phone switched off. Shit. I leave a cryptic message.

'It's me. We need to rearrange our date. Call me.'

What am I going to do if I can't get hold of him? What if he just turns up? I suppose Carly will have to come with me, which isn't the end of the world because it'll only be for a couple of days. Simone really will go apeshit, but at least it'll make her pay too. I wonder if I need to go and get any of Carly's things but then realise if it's to look like an authentic kidnapping, then I can't. She'll have to go as she is, in her pyjamas with the blanket wrapped around her. If I bring my phone, she can watch videos on that, and I'll make sure she's okay. But now I'm really on edge. I don't know if the plan is still on or whether Tony will delay things and not turn up. I can't keep my eyes off my watch. We agreed 8.30 pm would be the best time when I'd be the only person in the house, but time goes so slowly when you're watching it. Carly's eyes close, and her head lolls against my arm, and before I know it, her thumb has fallen out of her mouth, and she's breathing steadily and quite loudly. I try calling Tony again, but it still goes to voicemail. Minnie jumps up on the sofa next to me, and although she's not allowed to, I don't care. I stroke her rhythmically to settle my nerves.

I walk into the kitchen to get a drink, putting my phone on the table as I open the fridge.

And then it happens. I glance at the clock. It's twenty-five minutes past eight. I hear the unlocked front door swing open and heavy footsteps come running down the hall towards the living room. Why am I so stupid? I should have locked the door, and then they wouldn't have got in. I race out of the kitchen into the hall, ready to talk to Tony, but to my surprise, I see two men wearing balaclavas and black clothes storm into the living room.

'What are you doing?' I ask, standing in the doorway. In a split second, the tall guy throws a black blindfold around my head, squeezing it tightly, compressing my eyes. Minnie barks maniacally.

'Hey, guys, we need to delay this. I'm babysitting tonight. I tried to get hold of you, Tony, but you didn't answer. Didn't you get my message?'

I hear Carly wake up, and then she starts crying. 'Rose,' she says, but I can't see where she is.

'Let go of me, guys.' I try to reach upwards to remove the blindfold, but the man is too strong, and he bashes my arm away. I yelp with pain. I know this was meant to look authentic, but this is ridiculous.

'Take this thing off me, Tony. We need to delay.'

'What should I do, boss?' the man who is holding me asks. He's got a foreign accent, and his breath is hot and horrible against my ear. There's no answer from Tony, and all I can hear are Carly's sobs, which are getting louder and louder. I struggle, but the man grabs both of my arms and pulls them behind me, binding my wrists with something that feels like hard plastic and digs into my skin. 'Stop it!' I yell. 'We need to delay!'

The next thing I hear is the shattering of glass, things crashing all around me, and I realise with dismay that they're smashing the room up. Minnie is barking and barking.

'No! This has gone too far!' I shout. 'You're not meant to break things. Please don't hurt Carly or the dog.'

And then he locks his arm around my neck and puts duct tape around my mouth. I feel like I'm going to choke to death and have to remind myself to breathe through my nose. Minnie's barks become quieter, and I hope that it's just because someone has picked her up and carried her into the kitchen. I can still hear her yapping away. At least they haven't hurt her, or at least I pray they haven't. Tony wouldn't do something like that. We agreed that no one would get injured.

'Move.' The tall man with the foreign accent shoves me in my back, and with my wrists tied together behind me, I have no choice but to do as he says. I try to kick him, but he just laughs and tightens his arm around my neck. I can't even talk now. I hear Carly's snuffles from behind, and now I'm terrified. This doesn't feel right. Not at all. The next thing I know, the bitter night air hits my face, and I'm being forced into a cold metal trunk. Everything is black. The blindfold around my eyes is too tight, and no light leaks through. Carly is whimpering, and I edge closer to her so that her little body is encircled by mine. I wish I could stroke her hair, tell her that it's all okay. But it isn't. This wasn't meant to happen. The man grabs my ankles and holds them together, putting some plastic tie around them that digs into my flesh. And then a door is slammed shut, and I try to shift around, but my feet are up against hard metal.

The engine starts up, and we're thrown from side to side as the vehicle drives away. What the hell is Tony playing at? He never said anything about tying me up, chucking me into a car or a van. This was meant to be a bit of a laugh not a real kidnapping. I feel terrible, because it's one thing me being put in this situation, but little Carly doesn't deserve this. I just pray that whenever we get to wherever we're going, they'll take the tape off, and I can tell Carly that it's just a silly prank that we're playing, and we'll be home the day after tomorrow.

21

GOLDIE

Not only was the flight back from Milan completely full, it was also delayed by two hours, which meant my normal driver couldn't collect me from Heathrow. Thank goodness for Simone. By the time I'm through customs, my head feels like it's going to split in two. Unusually, I couldn't gauge how well the meeting went. The men in suits seemed to like the film proposal and thought they might have some investors who could bite, but until a contract is signed and the money is in the bank, I have to assume it's not going to happen. At least no one seemed to have heard about the rumours of drugs on set during our last film. That's a huge relief because I think Braun has been avoiding me, or at least avoiding having the conversation. He's barely been home, and of course he knew I had to go away. But tonight I'm going to discuss it with him whether he likes it or not.

I wave at Simone as I walk towards her, pulling my overnight case behind me.

'Thanks for collecting me,' I say.

'Sure.'

'Is everything alright with the kids? Did Florian get away okay?'

'Yes, all's fine although he really didn't want to go. Rose is at home, babysitting Carly.'

I sense that Simone wants to say something else, but she holds back. I hope my boy is alright. He's such a sensitive soul in a harsh world, and despite the way it breaks my heart to see him suffer, I know he has to toughen up at some point.

'Would you like to drive?' Simone asks as we approach the car in the multi-storey car park.

'No, I'm too tired. You drive.'

She nods, and we get in the car. When we're out of Heathrow and on the A30, Simone clears her throat. Her fingers are tightly gripped around the steering wheel.

'I'm sorry, Goldie, but I have to give my notice.'

It feels like the breath has been knocked out of me. I know that's an overreaction, but Simone is a godsend, so good at her job, and I can't bear the thought of being without her, especially now with all this pressure on me. And then, to make matters worse, I remember that I never actually gave Simone an employment contract or non-disclosure agreement, which means she's not even bound by any notice period. I suppress a groan.

'Did something happen?' I turn to look at her. Simone tenses her shoulders, and I wonder what Rose has done now. Our daughter is totally out of control, and I think we're going to need to consult a psychologist about her behaviour.

'No, nothing in particular. It's just little Carly and her father need me, and that's not compatible with having a full-time live-in job.'

I don't believe her. Simone's words are unconvincing, and I'm sure that Rose must have done something.

'Are you certain I can't persuade you to stay? More money perhaps?'

Simone shakes her head. 'No, I've made up my mind.'

'In which case please, please can you stay on for another fortnight at least, just so I can find someone else to fill your position.'

Simone hesitates.

I don't like to beg, but I say, 'Please,' again.

'Okay,' she says reluctantly. 'I'll stay on for another two weeks.'

'Thank you,' I reply, desperately hoping I can find a decent replacement.

We drive the rest of the journey in an awkward silence. Part of me wants to ask the real reason for her leaving, but the other part isn't sure I want to hear the answer. Besides, I get the feeling that Simone won't tell me.

I KNOW something is wrong the moment we pull into the drive. The front door is slightly ajar. Surely Rose wouldn't have left the door open with Carly in the house?

We glance at each other, and I see my panic mirrored in Simone's eyes. I rush out of the car, leaving the car door open, my bags inside. But in the doorway, I come to a halt, my breath catching in my throat.

'Hello?' I shout. 'Rose, are you home?'

I'm met with silence. And then I hear Minnie barking. It's manic, and it sounds like she's scratching a door. I open the front door fully and instantly know something terrible has happened. The vase on the hall table is lying shattered with shards of glass on the floor, the roses scattered around as if they've been thrown on a coffin. I gasp and hear Simone's intake of breath at my side. Time stops as I walk into the living room. The room has been destroyed. Picture frames lie shattered on the carpet, cushions ripped open with feathers settled everywhere, even the coffee table is on its side. But the thing I notice first is the big piece of paper attached with Sellotape to the picture above the fireplace. Written in thick black marker pen in capital letters, the words read:

DON'T CALL THE POLICE OTHERWISE YOUR DAUGHTER WILL DIE.

I sink down onto the floor, my hand over my mouth. Someone has taken Rose.

And then Simone starts shouting for Carly, and I realise that Rose was meant to have been babysitting Carly, which means either Carly is here, or she's been taken too. I let out a moan as I hear Simone's footsteps running downstairs, shouting her niece's name over and over. As I'm hauling myself up and backing out of the wrecked room, Simone reappears with Minnie in her arms. The dog is shivering and whimpering.

'She's not here. Carly's gone too. Minnie was locked in the kitchen.'

'Oh my God, what are we going to do?' I say, my trembling hand over my mouth.

'This is the only room that's been destroyed. Everywhere else is intact. What am I going to tell Rob?' There are tears in Simone's eyes, and I'm sure her white face reflects my own.

'I'll try calling Rose's phone. Maybe they've gone to the police station,' I suggest.

But our eyes are drawn back to the note on the picture, so I don't hold out much hope. I grab the landline and call Rose's number. It rings, but then there's an echoing ring. Both Simone and I rush towards the kitchen, where the ring of her phone gets louder and louder. It's lying there on the kitchen table, next to Carly's beaker of juice. I pick up my daughter's phone, but mine is the only missed call. I need to get into her phone to see whether she's tried calling anyone else, but I don't know her code.

'I'm so sorry, Simone. If I hadn't asked you to come to get me from the airport, this wouldn't have happened. You'd have been here, little Carly and Rose–' My voice breaks, and I sob. How can this even be happening? Kidnapping is the sort of thing I might include in a film; it doesn't happen in real life.

'Where's Braun?' Simone asks, although there's a hardness to her voice.

I swipe my eyes and answer in a hiccuping voice. 'In the editing suite, I assume. Where he always is. I texted him to say I'd landed, but I haven't heard back.' I realise I left my bag and my phone in the car. 'I'm going outside,' I say, pointing to the driveway. Simone nods.

Where is my girl? Is she really in danger, and if so, what can we do to rescue her? Are the abductors serious about us not telling the police? Surely they wouldn't know if we contacted the police, would they? Everything is so quiet outside, and all I can hear is my ragged, heavy breathing and footsteps as I walk to the car. The floodlight outside comes on, and I wonder whether any of our neighbours saw anything. I grab my handbag and small wheelie case and lock the car. I open the garage door and realise with a start that Braun's car is here. Surely he wasn't taken too? Wouldn't the note on the picture have said something to that effect?

Back inside the house, I'm worried about contaminating any evidence, but then realise that if we can't tell the police, that doesn't make any difference. I fish my mobile out of my bag. There are no missed calls and no text messages from Braun. I try calling him, and it goes straight to voicemail. What should I say? I can't leave him a message to say that Rose has been kidnapped. I hang up and then immediately call him again.

'Braun, you need to ring me now. Get home as quickly as

you can. There's been an emergency.' I then send him a text message to the same effect. I then call Martin. Hopefully he'll have left his phone on, especially as it's getting late now. In fact, thinking about it, why would Braun be with Martin this late anyway?

Martin answers on the second ring.

'Hi, Goldie.'

'Is Braun with you?'

'No, should he be?'

'Was he with you earlier?' There's a long hesitation. 'You need to tell me the truth!'

'What's the reprobate done this time?' Martin asks, but his laugh sounds forced.

'We have a family emergency, and his phone is switched off.'

'We were editing this morning, and then he left. Sorry, but I don't know where he is.'

'He didn't say anything?'

'I thought he was going home,' Martin explains.

'If he gets in touch, can you contact me immediately and tell him to come home?' I ask.

'Sure. And if there's anything I can do, please let me know.'

Where has he been all afternoon? I thought he understood the urgency of getting the edits finished.

What now? Simone comes into the hallway, a haunted look on her face. 'I think we should call the police anyway, or perhaps I could go to the police station, as they might not be tracking me.'

'Oh God, Simone. I don't know. I need to talk to Braun. He's better in emergency situations than me.'

I notice a flicker of doubt on Simone's face, but then she doesn't know my husband like I do. He's always been calm in emergencies, like the time that Rose caught her finger in the patio doors and there was so much blood I thought I might faint.

'He was here earlier this afternoon,' Simone says, a frown between her eyebrows, 'but then he left. Where does he go to drink?' Simone asks. 'A pub, a bar, friends' houses?'

'Good point. The White Horse. I'll call them.' Surely he won't have been drinking all afternoon, not when there's so much to do.

The phone rings and rings; unsurprising for a busy evening in a popular London pub. Eventually a young woman answers, and after much persuading, she agrees to look for Braun. Just when I'm about to give up, he comes onto the phone.

'Jeez, Goldie. You have to track me down to the pub. Since when did you get so desperate?' He's slurring his words slightly, and I can just see him there, my handsome husband, propping up the bar, the famous film director, just a little bit too pleased with himself. But it's still a massive relief to hear his voice. At least Braun is alright.

'You need to come home. Something terrible's happened.'

'What?'

'Just come home. Now.'

FIFTEEN MINUTES LATER, Braun steps into the hallway. 'What the hell?' he asks as he tries but fails to navigate his way around the shards of glass. 'Have we been burgled?'

'Not exactly.' He smells of beer and cigarette smoke. I take his arm and lead him into the living room.

'God,' he says as he reads the note on the wall. And then he steadies himself. 'This will be another of Rose's pranks.'

'Carly's gone too,' I say.

We stare at each other. Yes, Rose might do something stupid like this to get back at us, but we both know our daughter well enough to be convinced she would never do anything to hurt a little child. She was so sweet with Carly, a changed character around her.

'I think we should call the police,' Simone says. Braun jumps slightly as if he'd forgotten she was here.

'No. If they really have been kidnapped, we'll be receiving a ransom demand soon enough. If we go to the police, then it might put the girls in more danger. I don't think we can ignore that note.' We all stare at the piece of paper, as if the words might reveal some further hidden meaning, a riddle perhaps that will help us find the girls.

'We have to do something,' I say. Simone has sat down now, perched on the edge of an armchair that is undamaged, her head in her hands.

'We're going to have to sit tight until we hear from the kidnappers,' Braun insists.

I glance at Simone, but she doesn't meet my eyes. I sense that there's something she's not telling me, but I've no idea what.

22

SIMONE

I have never felt so terrified, so very sick to my stomach. This is all my fault. I was responsible for Carly, and now that innocent little girl, who has been through so much loss already in her short life, is in terrible danger. What's worse is I never told Rob the truth as to where she and I have been staying. Will I have to tell him now? He'll be devastated and rightly so. I've lied to him and put his daughter's life at peril. My moral duty is to tell Rob, but what if he goes to the police? If I were him, I would. I've failed him and Ally, and I've simply no idea what to do about it. Rose is a complicated girl, and yes, she could have got involved in something she shouldn't, and Carly could be collateral damage. On the other hand, Goldie and Braun are high profile and wealthy. Their offspring would make perfect targets for kidnappers. My thoughts are in turmoil. I should have got out of this place after I was pushed into the road. The events are likely unconnected, but I got a bad feeling then, and now Braun knows that I'm a fraud and I forged my CV. Is this some sort of payback by him?

I stare at him. He looks a mess: his hair on end, eyes

bloodshot, his face so pale it's almost grey. No, he looks genuinely shocked. He's hugging Goldie now, and she's crying silent tears onto his shoulder. At least they have each other. I've got no one. I think for a moment about Mark, my ex. I pushed him away when the relationship wasn't going anywhere, when I found him, frankly, boring. It was almost a relief that he had been cheating on me. For the first time, I have a feeling of regret. I want arms around me; I want to be comforted and to be told that everything will be alright. Yet, I feel pity for Goldie. Does she know that her husband is a sleaze? I want to leave this house now, yet I can't. I have to find Carly.

'What are we going to do?' Goldie says, stepping away from her husband, clutching her arms around her skinny frame. She walks towards the kitchen, and Braun follows. I go after them, trying to avoid catching Braun's eyes. He repulses me.

He pours himself a brandy and holds up the bottle. 'It's not the good stuff, but it'll have to do. Do you want a glass?' He directs the question to Goldie and me. We both decline.

And then the phone rings. The landline. All three of us freeze. The only people who call on the landline are Braun's parents, yet none of us think it's likely to be them. It rings three times before Braun comes out of his reverie. 'I'll answer it,' he says as he walks towards the phone and picks it up. He immediately puts it on loudspeaker. For that I'm grateful.

'Yes.'

The voice is mechanical and monotone, distorted, I assume, by a computer or an app. 'We want one million pounds in cash. If you go to the police, the girls will be harmed. Do you understand?'

'Yes,' Braun says quietly.

'You'll be told where to come with the money in forty-eight hours from now.'

'Wait! Where's Rose? Where's Carly?' Goldie rushes towards the phone, which Braun is holding out in front of him, as if it's contaminated. His hand is shaking, and I can't tell if it's from the alcohol or fear; perhaps both.

But there's no reply to Goldie's questions. The person has hung up.

'Can you see who dialled the number?' Goldie asks. 'Press 1471.'

Braun does as he's told. The automated voice says, 'This number has not been recognised.'

We all stare at the phone.

'A million pounds!' Braun exclaims. 'That's a joke. How can we get a million pounds together?'

Goldie opens and closes her mouth. At least they're not looking at me because a million pounds is so beyond my reach it's laughable. The last time I looked, I had three thousand four hundred pounds in my bank account, and I thought I was doing pretty well with my savings. I used all the money inherited from our parents on purchasing my little maisonette.

'Even if we can get hold of it, we can't get it in forty-eight hours,' Goldie says. 'It's impossible. And to get that amount of cash, it's a joke. They must know it's not possible. But we've got to do it, Braun. This is Rose's life at stake. We have to!'

'And Carly's,' I say, but they both ignore me.

'Is this even for real?' Braun repeatedly runs his fingers through his hair and starts pacing the kitchen, but he's not walking in straight lines. I think he's still drunk.

'Have you got CCTV?' I ask. I know there's an alarm system because I have to switch it on and off every time I leave and enter the house, but I haven't seen any cameras. Not that the Deluccis would tell me about them.

'Yes!' Goldie exclaims, slapping the side of her head. 'It's only a cheap camera we got off Amazon, but it's on the drainpipe at the front of the house. We've got the video doorbell, but that only records when someone presses it.'

I'm surprised they don't have a more sophisticated system, living in such luxury in a beautiful part of London.

'It's on your phone, Braun. We need to have a look.'

Braun takes his phone out of his back pocket and fumbles with it. 'Can't remember the password.'

'For God's sake,' Goldie says, taking it from him. She punches in various passwords, holds the phone up to Braun's face for facial recognition, and then she's in the app. I don't want to stand too close to Braun, but I have to see this.

'It's there!' Goldie exclaims. 'Look, just before 8.30 pm.'

This isn't a joke. This isn't one of Rose's scams. A white van reverses rapidly up the drive to the front of the house and positions itself in such a way that we can't see the number plate. But it's dark, and I doubt we'd have been able to make it out anyway. Two people exit the van. They're wearing black from head to toe, balaclavas hiding their faces and covering their hair. But once they're through the front door, there's no further movement because the camera faces away from the house.

And then less than ten minutes later, they're coming out of the door, and this time one of them is pulling Rose. She has a blindfold around her head, and her wrists are bound, but she's still trying to kick and punch the person who is holding her. It's horrifying to watch, especially as she seems to be inflicting little damage to this tall, burly intruder. I gasp when I see Carly. She doesn't have a blindfold on, but the person carrying her has his or her hand over Carly's mouth. She looks so tiny and vulnerable, dressed in her pyjamas, her pink furry slippers on her feet and a blanket wrapped around her shoulders. It's so quick because both girls are quickly bundled into the back of the van before it races off.

'No!' Goldie exclaims.

'Play it again,' Braun says. Goldie hands him the phone.

'I thought it might be some kind of wind-up, the sort of thing Rose might think was funny, but this is the real deal, isn't it?' Braun mutters, his voice choked.

'Can you pause the video when they go into the house?' I ask. I'm standing so close to Braun now, and I have to stop myself from breathing in his rancid beer breath. Braun does as I ask, but it's impossible to tell anything. The light is too poor, the quality of the video grainy.

'What are we going to do?' Goldie asks in a whisper. She looks utterly lost, waif-like.

'I'm going to ask my parents for the money,' Braun says, shoving his phone into his jeans pocket.

'What are you going to say to them? Will you tell them what's happened because your mum, well, she talks, doesn't she? And have they even got that much money? They've invested loads in the business.'

'I don't know, but it's our best hope. Leave it with me. Stay here. Lock the doors and call me if anything happens.' And then Braun swivels around and walks out of the kitchen. A few seconds later, I hear his car start up.

I wonder what Braun's parents do to have that much wealth. It's unfathomable to me.

'He's over the limit,' Goldie cries as she lays her head down on the table. 'What if he has an accident? Or what if he gets picked up by the police? What then?'

'I'm sure he'll be fine,' I try to reassure her, but Braun is hot-headed, and Goldie is right. Braun has drunk much too much this evening. I wonder if he's taken drugs too. 'Where do his parents live?'

'Barnes.'

At least that's not too far away, and hopefully he'll drive sensibly; as sensibly as he can under the circumstances. And then I think about Braun and how he's in so much debt. Why is he in so much debt if his parents are loaded? I suppose he can't just go running to the bank of Mum and Dad at his age, but that's not stopping him now. What did he borrow that money for? I wonder if it's to pay off a woman he's harassed, a woman like me who might have succumbed to his advances and then regretted it. Could that have happened to Ally? Or is he involved in this scam somehow? Would he organise the kidnap of his own daughter to raise funds from his parents? Surely even Braun wouldn't stoop that low. But I don't trust him one iota. And then there's the real worry that Braun knows my references are faked. Have his investigations gone one step further, and does he know who I really am? Should I be scared of Braun, and am I next to be kidnapped or worse? But then I recall his white face and horrified reaction when he learned of his daughter's abduction, and I doubt that even if he is an excellent actor, which indeed he might be since he's surrounded by them every day, he could fake that reaction. All I know is that Carly's fate is in the hands of strangers and the Deluccis, and I don't trust them one bit. Worse than that, this is of my own making. I should never have brought Carly here. I say a silent prayer both to God and my angel sister Ally, asking for Carly's safe return and for forgiveness. Right now I would give my life for Carly's. This is all my fault, and I'm such a fool.

23

ROSE

I twist my body around so that my bound hands can stroke Carly's hair, but it's ineffectual and hurts me, so in the end I just wrap my body around hers the best I can. I wish I could talk to her, but with this tape around my mouth all I can emit are grunting sounds, and I don't want to scare Carly further. Her tears are soaking my cheeks, and she clings to me, yet I can't give her any comfort in return. I think we're in the back of a van, as it smells of diesel and wet dog, and we're thrown from side to side as the vehicle turns. I can't see a thing, and time means nothing. It makes me realise how hard it must be being blind, how much I rely on my eyes for everything. I can't even tell how long we're in here for. From time to time I try kicking my legs at the metal, which may or may not be the sides of the vehicle or the doors, but all it does is hurt me.

I know I agreed with Tony that the kidnapping should look authentic, but this is ridiculous. I can't decide whether this is Tony doing his job properly or whether something else is going on here. Why did they have to bring Carly, and why didn't he take on board my message when I said we needed to take a rain check?

Eventually the vehicle comes to a standstill, and I hear two doors open and slam shut, the reverberations shuddering through me. Cold air hits us as the rear doors are opened, but I can't see a thing.

'Get out,' a man says, grabbing me by the feet. I try to kick out at him, but he's too strong, and my ankles are tied together. I hear scissors snipping through the ties, and then I'm hauled to my feet. 'Walk,' he says. I feel all wobbly because I can't use my arms for balance and have no idea which way is up. I try to speak, but my voice is completed muffled.

He grabs my arm and pulls me forwards. My legs and feet are numb with pins and needles, and it's hard to get them to move properly. I stumble, and he rights me, but his fingers dig deep into the flesh of my arms, and I'm sure I'll have bruises. I try to whimper, but no sound comes out.

'Don't try anything, or the little one will be killed, and you'll be next.' I shudder. Why is he saying this? It's not like he needs to, unless of course Tony hasn't told this guy the truth. Unless he thinks this kidnapping is for real.

'Walk up the stairs.'

He pushes me upwards, up two or three flights, or even more perhaps, his hand on my back, my shoulder rubbing along the cold, rough wall. Then we're on level ground, and I'm shoved forwards again. I listen out for Carly. Where is she? What have they done with her?

'Stand still and don't move.'

He tugs off my blindfold, and all I see are stars and light that is too bright. I blink rapidly until eventually my vision returns and I can focus. In fact, it's not light in here at all; it's barely lit up. I'm in a big space with high ceilings, an industrial warehouse or something. There are exposed steel girders and tall windows that are cut up into smaller panes with black metal. The place is deserted. Detritus is scattered on the concrete floor – old sweet wrappers, a couple of office chairs, one of which is lying on its side, the wheels missing, crumpled up bits of paper – and a single strip light hangs from wires in the centre of the room. It flickers a bit, which just adds to the creepiness of this place. And then the man whips the tape off my mouth, burning my skin, making me gasp with pain.

I rub my face to ease the soreness and then turn to look at him. I don't recognise the form of this tall, stocky man dressed from head to toe in black, a woollen balaclava covering his head.

'Tell Tony he didn't need to bring us here. We could have gone to a hotel or his home. This isn't necessary.'

The man swipes my face, catching the side of my cheek with an ugly gold ring. 'Shut up!' he says menacingly, and I stagger backwards. 'Do you want to keep those ties on your wrists?'

'No,' I say, my voice trembling.

'Then shut your face and hold your arms out.' I can't work out his accent.

I do as I'm told, and he takes a knife, slicing through the plastic tie.

The door opens again, and another man wearing black clothes and a balaclava comes in, carrying Carly. He puts her on the floor. I bend down, hold out my sore arms, and Carly races into them, flinging her hands around my neck, her little body convulsing in sobs. The first man who manhandled me coughs up phlegm and spits it out onto the floor before walking out through the black door.

I look up at the second man, and despite his balaclava and black clothes, I know exactly who he is. I've looked into those beautiful blue eyes too many times before, put my arms around his waist as we've sped through London.

'Tony, what are you doing? This isn't necessary. You know this doesn't have to be real. We could stay in a hotel, and no one would be any the wiser.'

He laughs then. He actually laughs, but he still says nothing. It's not a laugh I recognise. It's mean and hard, and I wonder in a moment of horrible realisation whether I've got Tony totally wrong.

'Talk to me, Tony,' I say, but he just shakes his head.

'Why are you doing this? It isn't part of our plan.'

After a long silence he sighs. 'Might not be part of your plan, but it's very much part of mine.' How could I have been so stupid? Tony who was so sweet to me, who helped me hone my craft, who flirted with me and made me feel wanted, who called me his partner, he's lied to me. Has he used me all of this time? Or is this opportunistic?

'Did you want to keep all of the ransom money for yourself because if that's what this is about, then you can have my share. But please let Carly go. She shouldn't be here, and you don't need to keep me a prisoner. Not like this.'

His face stretches outwards, and I can tell that he's grinning underneath that hideous balaclava, that he thinks my words are funny.

I wonder whether I could attack him, throw myself onto him, poke his eyes out, the only body parts I can actually see, but who am I kidding? Tony is strong. He works out and has bulging muscles. He'd overpower me in seconds.

I glance around the space again and for the first time notice a mattress shoved into the corner of the room.

'Come on, sweetheart,' I say, picking Carly up and walking over to the stained, bare mattress. There's a metal bowl in the corner along with a couple of bottles of water and some chocolate bars. A shiny blue sleeping bag is rolled up in the corner. I can feel Tony's eyes on me, so I pull my shoulders back and walk as straight as I can. If Carly weren't with me, I'd tell him where to shove it.

I sit Carly on the mattress and plonk myself down next to her, pulling her into my arms. She's sucking her thumb and fiddling with her blanket.

'How long are you planning on keeping us here?'

Tony doesn't answer me. Instead, he turns around and strides out, slamming the black door behind him. The sound of a key in the lock fills me with horror.

'I need to go for pee pee,' Carly whispers.

'Okay, sweetie. Let me find out where there's a loo,' I say. I haul myself up from the mattress and stride to the door. I try the handle although I don't know why I bother because Tony just locked it. Then I kick the door repeatedly.

'You need to let us out so we can go to the toilet,' I shout.

I can hear men's voices on the other side, but they don't respond to me.

I thump the door again and wriggle the handle up and down.

'We need the loo!' I yell.

Footsteps get louder, and I stand back slightly in case it swings open. 'Use the bowl. That's what it's there for,' Tony says.

'Why are you doing this to me, Tony? I thought we were friends.'

I get no response.

AFTER HELPING Carly pee in the bowl, I give her a drink of water from one of the bottles and suggest she lie down on the mattress. I put her blanket over her and stroke her hair. Just as she's settling, the door flings open, and the two men pace back in. I don't know why Tony's bothering with keeping his balaclava on because I know it's him, and he knows that I do. He takes out his phone.

'Prop her up, and both of you look at me.' He holds out a newspaper.

'Take it.'

I do as I'm told because at least it'll be something to read.

Carly's eyes have sprung open, and she looks at me, terror in her little face.

'Why?' I ask.

'Why do you think, idiot?' the other man says. 'We need your photographs to prove we've got you, obviously.' He turns to Tony. 'You didn't tell me she was thick as well as butt ugly.'

I feel like I'm going to explode with anger. I want to jump up, throw my fist into both of their faces, but I know that's not going to work. I don't know what these two are capable of, but I can't risk anything, for Carly's sake.

'Hold the newspaper up so we can see the date. Say cheese!' Tony says as he takes a photograph of us. Then he grabs the paper from me, sticking it under his arm. Once again, they both turn around and stride out of the door, locking it behind them.

24

Goldie and I don't know what to do. She wanted to start clearing up the house, but I've stopped her. If we do call the police, there'll be evidence here. I want to get out onto the streets to start searching for Carly and Rose, but I've no idea where to go, where to start looking. And so we sit in the kitchen, drinking sugary cups of tea, watching the clock's hand move painfully slowly.

'Why isn't Braun back yet?' Goldie murmurs. It's nearly 1 am, and he's been gone for almost two hours. Goldie tries calling him, but he doesn't answer.

'Do you think he's been picked up by the police?' she asks.

I shrug. 'It's not like you can ring them to find out. Perhaps you could call his parents and find out what time he left their house.'

Goldie hesitates. 'It's so late. I'll be waking them.'

I think that's a strange comment. I can't imagine any loving grandparents would be getting much sleep knowing their granddaughter has been kidnapped.

'What's the problem?' I ask, because frankly I haven't got time for any niceties.

'They don't like me very much, Braun's parents. I'm the girl from the working-class background who stole their son. And Braun persuaded them to invest in Delucci Productions, so we owe them a lot of money.'

I wonder if Braun owes his parents money personally as well.

'Surely none of that matters at a time like this?'

'Thinking about it, I'm surprised Braun even suggested going to his parents. He's proud, you know. He hates having to ask them for money.'

'But this is different.'

'You're right,' she says reluctantly, and dials their number. I can hear the phone ringing and ringing. Just when I think both Goldie and I are about to lose hope, a male voice comes onto the line.

'Hello.'

'Gary, it's Goldie. Is Braun on his way home?'

'What? What do you mean, Goldie?'

'Has Braun left your house yet?'

'He wasn't here. I don't know what you're talking about, and anyway, why are you calling us in the middle of the night?'

I suppress a groan, and Goldie shrinks into herself. 'Didn't Braun arrive at your house about an hour or so ago?'

'No. What's going on? Have you two had an argument?'

'Of course not, it's nothing. He was just on his way over. Sorry to have woken you. We'll talk in the morning.' And then she ends the call.

'Why didn't you say anything to them?'

'It's not my place, and now I'm worried that something has happened to Braun. Oh God, what are we going to do? Do you think he might have had an accident on the way over? I mean, he had certainly drunk too much and shouldn't have been driving. Shall I call around the hospitals just in case?'

'No, Goldie. I'm sure there's an explanation; after all, it's not the first time that Braun has disappeared without trace, is it?'

Goldie frowns at me, and I wonder if I've said too much. It's not like I have any great insight into his marriage, but I'm sure I'm not the first person Braun has come onto, and a philanderer is going to have a suitcase full of excuses. 'It's just that he wasn't available earlier, and you were worried, but it turns out he was at the pub. I tried to reach him before Florian went on his trip, but he didn't answer my calls. I expect Braun is cruising the streets, looking for the girls, and has the sound switched off on his phone.'

'But his parents are our only hope of getting the money.'

'What about your business? You're doing well, aren't you?' I suggest.

Goldie groans. 'The only way that I can possibly pay the ransom is by robbing Delucci Productions' business account, and I'd be stealing all of our investors' money. It would ruin us.'

'It would ruin you!' I thump my fist on the table. I can't help it. Anger pulses through my veins. I stand up and start pacing the kitchen. 'Who cares if it ruins you! Your daughter's and my niece's lives are on the line here, and you need to get the money from wherever you can. Your life is a mess, Goldie, and Carly has been caught in the crossfire.'

I run my fingers through my hair and think of my sister. The chances are that Ally was caught in the Deluccis' mess, and now Carly and I are too. I've seen enough of Goldie to believe that she's innocent, but Braun, on the other hand, I don't believe for one second he is. I can't prove it, but I will. I have to. Perhaps the time has come to tell Goldie the truth.

'Has your husband told you about me?' I stand with my hands on my hips.

'Told me what?'

'That my CV is faked.'

Goldie's mouth falls open, and I actually feel sorry for her. Her head has been so buried in her beloved business, she's been blind to everything that's going on around her. Now is the time for truth.

'My name is Simone Carver, and Alison Greystone was my sister.'

'What?' Goldie is trembling now, and if circumstances were different, I'd pull her into a hug.

'Was it a coincidence that you got this job? Did you come back to the UK because she died?'

'No. I got this job because I was opportunistic, because I wanted to find out more about you and Braun, to know why my sister died driving your car, why she had drugs in her system.'

'I don't understand,' she whispers.

'Didn't you think Ally's death was suspicious, Goldie?'

'Well, of course I did, but the police investigated.' Her voice fades away.

'The thing is, you don't see a single thing that's going on right in front of your eyes. Do you know what your husband is really like? Do you know that he's a sex pest, that he tried it on with me in your marital bedroom only a few hours ago? That's one of the reasons I handed in my notice. Have you decided to turn a blind eye to his behaviour, or are you just in denial?'

Goldie whimpers under her breath, but I'm on a roll and can't stop.

'And did you know that he's seriously in debt? Why is he so overdrawn on an account in his name? And what about Rose? Did you know that she set Lauren up and planted your belongings in Lauren's room? We both know that she tried to do the same to me, but I found the bottles of alcohol and disposed of them before you searched my flat. Did you know she's seeing a man likely twice her age? Then there's poor Florian, who was desperate not to go on the school trip and who is being horribly bullied at school and is probably dyslexic, yet too ashamed to tell you anything, too worried to upset his busy mum. You don't know anything at all about your family, do you?'

Goldie stares at me, stock-still for a second, and then with tears in her eyes, she cries, 'Shut up, Simone! Just shut up!'

It's as if I've lanced something truly horrible, and she just sobs her heart out. And yes, now I do feel terrible, because not only has her daughter been kidnapped, her house ransacked and her husband is missing, I've just articulated some immensely painful home truths. The woman looks broken.

I groan. Perhaps now wasn't the time or the place, but it's too late. I pull out the chair next to where Goldie's sitting and put my arm around her shuddering shoulders.

'I'm sorry,' I say.

She sniffs. 'I'm sorry too,' she says in a hiccupped voice. 'You've been caught up in our mess. And the problem is, you're right about everything.' She sobs again.

After rubbing her back for a bit, I stand up and pour her a glass of water. We could both do with a stiff drink, but I'm not going into the trashed living room to find us something stronger.

'Why are you here, Simone?' she asks eventually.

'I thought you or Braun might have had something to do with Ally's death.'

'But we didn't.' She stares at me with a bewildered expression.

'I know you didn't.' I let my words peter out. 'The thing is, Goldie, do you think that Braun could have had something to do with the kidnap of the girls? It's just that I stumbled across some bank statements that suggest he's in debt by tens of thousands of pounds, and now he's gone AWOL. It's all a bit strange, isn't it?'

She tries calling his mobile phone again, but once more it rings out.

'I don't think Braun would do anything to endanger Rose. He adores her.'

I'm inclined to agree, but that doesn't mean he hasn't got anything to do with this mess.

25

GOLDIE

I've always prided myself on being strong, on being the backbone of our family, yet now I realise that it's been an illusion. For years, my focus has been Delucci Productions. It was my dream, my idea, my project, and Braun just came along for the ride. He's a reasonable director, but I've been the driving force behind everything, so eager to be the successful career woman, to prove that despite coming from nothing, I could be something. Be someone. And that I could prove Braun's parents wrong. That just because I didn't go to a private school and I was brought up by my single mother and didn't mix in the right circles, I couldn't rise to the top. But at what price? My ambition is nothing compared to my family, and why has it taken this for me to realise it?

I need to be alone, away from this woman who has infiltrated our household and has suffered such grief herself.

'I'm going to take a shower,' I say, standing up and wiping my face with my sleeve. 'And then we'll have to regroup. Decide what we're going to do next. Perhaps we should try to get a few hours' sleep, although I doubt I'll be able to.'

'Fair enough,' Simone says. 'I might try to lie down for a little while. If anything happens, please wake me.'

'You know, I'm very sorry about the loss of your sister. She was a great actress.'

Simone smiles weakly.

As I walk out of the room, my mobile phone clutched in my hand, and stride up the sweeping staircase, I look at our house. Really look. Not just pass through as I usually do. This is a beautiful home, with black and white cinematic pictures on the walls, pale oak floors and wide expanses of glass. The gentle scent of roses from the vase in the hall table envelops me. This home is pure luxury and had been beyond my wildest dreams, yet we're only here thanks to Braun's parents, not that I realised that for many years. Braun gave the impression that he had been highly successful as a banker before turning to film directing, and why would I have questioned that? But now I don't think Braun has been truthful. I think that his parents have bankrolled much of our lives, and I simply haven't realised. I've been so consumed by our films that I've neglected our children and probably our marriage too. How could I have been so blind? How could I have been such a terrible mother when all I wanted to do was give my children a stable family life, very different to my own childhood?

I walk into our bedroom and stare at the neatly made bed with the taupe wool throw and silk pillows. Did Braun really make a move on Simone in here? I shiver with disgust, wondering what else might have happened with other women in my absence. It's true that he has had numerous nights when he says he's been working late, and I've never checked up on him. Is it because I trusted him or because I don't really want to know the truth? Have I been burying my head in the sand for years?

But worse is the damage I've done to our children. I've

pretended that Rose's hard, bolshy exterior is her way of rebelling, that she's only acting as a typical teenager. The truth is I have no idea what's going on in my daughter's life. I walk into our luxurious pale limestone bathroom with its double sink and rainwater walk-in shower and turn on the tap. I strip off and step under the water, turning the heat right up. I need to feel the burning on my body to wash away some of the shame I feel for letting everyone down. And little Florian, my sensitive, gentle boy. I knew he didn't want to go on this school trip. I even forced him into doing football club and outdoor courses when he'd much rather stay at home and draw cartoons. Whom have I done that for? Braun probably, to turn our boy into the young man that my husband expects him to be. I allow myself to wail as the burning water pummels my head and back. I've failed everyone. Perhaps it's not too late for Florian. I can be the mother he deserves, but is it too late for Rose? What if they hurt her? What if I never see my daughter again? I crouch down in the shower. I cannot let that happen. I cannot fail her. The most important thing is to get Rose and Carly home, to make sure they know they are safe and loved. If it means ruining my business to achieve that, and it means I have to steal from my investors to save the lives of the girls, then so be it. I will willingly go to prison and pay for my crime because it means they'll be safe. Yes, my investors will be out of pocket, but no one invests in films unless they can afford to take the risk, because such investments are always risky. And when I'm out of prison, I'll work extra hard to pay them all back with interest, because that's what Rose and Carly deserve. Poor little Carly lost her mother, yet she has an aunt who was prepared to go to such lengths to discover how her sister died that she faked her way into our lives. The irony is, Simone is so much better at the job than Lauren was, yet she hasn't got the experience.

I turn the tap to cold because I want to shock myself to

stay awake, to truly focus on how we're going to find the girls, and then shivering violently, I wrap myself in a warm, fluffy towel and hurriedly get dry. It may be 2 am or some ungodly hour, but we have no time to lose.

I run back downstairs, expecting to have to go the basement to wake Simone, but she hears my footsteps and comes out of the kitchen.

'You didn't have a rest?' I ask.

She shakes her head. 'I wouldn't be able to sleep anyway, not under the circumstances.'

'A coffee, then?' I ask, dialling Braun's number yet again. There's still no answer.

'I'll make it,' Simone says.

'You know you said that Braun is in debt; how do you know?' I ask.

She grimaces. 'I'm sorry. I snooped. I looked in his briefcase and found some bank statements.'

'Can you show me?' It doesn't make sense because I manage all of our accounts both for home and Delucci Productions.

'Assuming his briefcase is still in the hall and the burglars didn't take it, yes.'

Simone puts two double espressos on the kitchen table, and I follow her out into the hallway towards the front door. Braun's briefcase is where he always leaves it, on the bench to the right side of the entrance lobby. It's hidden slightly, as a couple of pale grey cushions partially obscures it. Thank goodness it wasn't taken. She points to it. I step forwards and carry the briefcase back into the kitchen. I've never looked inside it except on the very rare occasion Braun asked me to fetch a script, and it's never crossed my mind to go through it. Why would I? I had no reason to suspect him. Except I should have, shouldn't I? Am I right to be doubting my husband on the say-so of this stranger? Now I'm not sure, but no harm will come from looking through his papers. I take a wodge and place them on the table.

'The statements are in there,' Simone says, pointing at a black plastic folder. I open it up and extract several bank statements. I sort them into date order, the most recent on top. As I look through the large numbers, I struggle to make sense of what I'm seeing. This account is in Braun's name only; it's an account I had no idea existed.

'Look, those are the outgoings, that's the bank interest, and that's the cumulative amount he owes. Do you recognise this bank account?' she asks.

I'm in shock. 'No. This is nothing to do with me, and what are these huge sums of money for? Who has he been paying out to?'

'I don't know, but it's not looking good.'

That's an understatement. From the numbers on this bank statement, it looks as if my husband has been siphoning large sums of money on a regular basis. But where has the money come from, and where is it going? What is he involved in? I thought he and I were partners, that we shared everything: our lives, our business, our shared dreams for our children and our future. Yet now, I wonder if I've been so single-minded in achieving success for Delucci Productions that I've totally misjudged my husband. He has always wanted to prove himself to his parents, whereas I just want financial security for my family, the financial security that I never had as a child.

When Dad walked out on Mum, I was twelve. He just disappeared one day. I only saw him again once, and that was fifteen years ago after Mum died. He tipped up wanting money. I told him to go to hell. At first, it was me and Mum against the world, but Mum preferred booze to me, and she slipped away from me too. My beloved grandmother stepped in, but she died too young. I thought Braun understood my overwhelming need to create security for us, that I wasn't bothered about the trappings of wealth or even the accolades that came with the success of our films. It was all about squirrelling money away for a rainy day so that our children would never have to experience what I went through. Yet it looks like Braun never truly understood. Unless he has set up a highly complicated financial scam, he isn't siphoning money from the business. I study Delucci Productions' banking every single day. So if these funds didn't come from our business, they must have come from Braun's parents or another source, one that I don't want to consider. Is Braun doing something illegal? It's as if Simone can read my mind.

'Now you've seen these, do you think he could be involved in the kidnapping?' Simone asks. 'Could he have set it up? I mean, it's really odd that he's just disappeared now.'

'I don't know,' I say. 'I just can't imagine it.' But then I couldn't imagine any of the things that Simone has told me; frankly, our lives are echoing a plot out of one of our films. It's like I'm living in some horrible alternative reality, and soon it will come to an end, and the audience will clap their approval, and the lights will come up, and the box office revenues will come pouring in, with great reviews and happy investors. Except it's not. If Simone is right and Braun has set up this 'kidnapping', then at least Rose and Carly will be safe. He may be a lying, conniving bastard, but one thing I am sure about is that he would never harm Rose. He adores our girl. But I'll be damned if I'm going to risk stealing from our investors to pay him. There is no way that my husband will receive the ransom money, directly or indirectly.

'What are we going to do?' Simone asks.

'I really don't know. But one thing is certain, we can't rely on anyone else. You and I need to find the girls ourselves. I don't know how, but we're going to have to figure it out.'

'First thing we need to do is try to work out who all of these people and companies he's been paying are,' I say.

'I don't recognise any of these names,' Goldie says, running her finger down the page of the most recent statement. She's clearly really shaken by the bank statements.

'This one. RNL Motors. He paid £18K for something last month. We should be able to work that one out?' I suggest. And then I wonder with a horrifying stab. Was that something to do with Ally's accident? Did he pay for a new car or work on the damaged one? But that doesn't make sense. Goldie's car was a write-off and worth a lot more than eighteen thousand pounds. They used the insurance payout to buy her new car. I've seen the accounts.

'Let's do a search for RNL Motors,' I suggest.

Goldie fetches the bags that she brought back from the airport and extracts her laptop. She fires it up and puts RNL Motors into Google. When the search loads, she angles the screen towards me.

'It's a motorbike dealership,' she murmurs. 'But why

would he be going there? Braun doesn't own a motorbike, and he's never been interested in having one. He's talked about a motorboat but not a bike.'

Then I remember the man lounging against his motorbike, the man who had come to take Rose out on the evening I banned her from leaving the house. He was a lot older than Rose. Could that be a coincidence?

'We can call them in the morning,' Goldie says. 'But right now, I don't suppose there's much we can do. I'll keep on trying to reach Braun.'

We agree to try to sleep for a couple of hours and reconvene at 7 am, assuming neither of us have heard anything prior to then. I expect Goldie will be ringing around hospitals to find out if Braun has been admitted anywhere; I just hope she avoids calling any police stations. I go downstairs to my flat, but of course I can't sleep. I am consumed with guilt and fear, silently begging forgiveness for putting Carly in this situation, terrified of how I'm going to tell Rob. I toss and turn and eventually give up trying to sleep.

We're both back in the kitchen well before 7 am. Goldie is still unable to reach Braun, and with her hair unbrushed and a pale face devoid of makeup, I can tell she's eaten up with fear for both her daughter and husband. At 8 am, Goldie telephones RNL Motors, putting her mobile on loudspeaker. The phone is answered by a gruff-sounding man, and in the background we can hear the revving of an engine.

'I'm calling regarding the purchase of a motorbike from you a month ago. I was wondering if I could check the ownership details.'

'If you bought it, then you know who owns it,' the man says.

'Yes, of course I know who owns it,' Goldie says. We should have practised this conversation before she picked up the phone. 'It's just I need to double-check the address you've got for the owner because it's a company transaction, and we need the information for our tax return.'

'Sorry, can't help.' It's obvious he's about to put the phone down.

'Actually, it was purchased by Braun Delucci, the film director, and I'm calling on behalf of Delucci Productions because we're interested in purchasing another bike from you. Just one second whilst I check the make and model with my assistant, but I believe they're very expensive. I'm Goldie Delucci, the producer and co-owner of Delucci Productions.'

I quickly type into Google 'expensive motorbike' and show the page to Goldie.

'Yes, it's a Honda RC213V-S Super Sport. I believe they cost well over one hundred thousand pounds. We're looking to purchase one for Brendan Fernsby, the Hollywood actor.'

We can both hear the intake of breath, and the man's attitude changes instantly. 'A lot more than a hundred grand. You said you're buying him one?'

'Yes. He's coming over from the States to film with us, and he wants the bike as part of his remuneration package. Braun Delucci recommended I contact you, as he'd like to put more business your way. He did something similar on the last purchase, buying the bike as part of the remuneration package for one of our actors.'

'Yes, I remember Mr Delucci now. He bought a Yamaha. So what was the first question you asked me?'

'Whether you could supply me with the ownership details of the Yamaha. As it's a company purchase, we need more information to give to our accountant.'

Goldie glances at me, and I give her the thumbs up because she's doing really well. I'm impressed.

'And how soon are you looking to purchase the Honda? Because obviously it's not a stock item.'

'Of course not. Just as soon as you can get hold of one,

and perhaps you could call back with the price and timescales. But in the meantime, if I could get the information for the Yamaha, please.'

'Right, well, I'll have to look through the records. Give me your number, and I'll get back to you.'

'It's urgent, Mr—'

'Roger Neil Langsford, it's me who owns the business.'

'Mr Langsford. As I mentioned, my name is Goldie Delucci, and I'd be very grateful if you could get back to me urgently.'

'Okay, I'll get back to you. And how soon do you need the Honda?'

'Yesterday, preferably,' Goldie says.

'The poor man is desperate for the business,' I remark after Goldie has ended the call.

'Yes, he wasn't very subtle about it. Let's just hope he calls us back quickly.'

Roger Neil Langsford does. He calls back within ten minutes, and I can almost see him salivating for our business.

'So, the bike is registered to a man called Anthony White of Flat 6, 17 Coulsby Avenue, London E37 7GH. Is that what you need?'

'That's fabulous, thank you,' Goldie says.

'I'll get back to you later with a quote for the Honda,' he says.

'I look forward to it.'

'Who is Anthony White?' I ask, turning to look at Goldie.

'I've absolutely no idea,' she replies. 'That name means nothing. I've no idea why Braun would be buying this man a bike. It just doesn't make sense.'

'There's only one thing we can do,' I suggest. 'Go and pay him a visit.'

. . .

WE LOCK UP THE HOUSE, which seems ironic considering we're leaving a scene of devastation in the hall and living room. Goldie insists on bringing Minnie with us. I think she's fearful that the house might be broken into again and the dog stolen. She plugs the address into her satnav and steers the car towards east London. It's rush hour, and we make very slow progress. Every twenty minutes or so, Goldie tries calling Braun, but his phone is never answered. We try to listen to the radio, but the news seems trite, and music is just wrong. In the end we sit there in silence.

We arrive in a run-down part of London, with block after block of concrete flats. Everything is grey: the buildings, the sky, the pavements. I keep a lookout for the red motorbike, but I don't see any bikes, just lots of cars parked along every road and pavement. And there are people, scores of them. Young mothers pushing prams, the elderly pulling shopping trolleys, a few youths huddled together smoking, and even a parking warden checking the parked cars.

'Over there,' I say, pointing out an apartment block with the number seventeen on its side. It's a squat, concrete building, smaller than many around here, and I count twelves doors, four on each of the three floors. 'As there's nowhere to park, shall I nip out and see if anyone's at home?' I suggest.

'Do you think it's safe?' Goldie asks. 'I mean safe for you to knock on his door?'

I sigh. I've no idea, but then there are lots of people around. It's not like it's the middle of the night. 'I'll give it a go,' I say.

'I know this area,' Goldie says.

'What?' My hand is on the door handle.

'I was brought up around here, a few streets over, but didn't have the easiest of starts.'

I'm dumbstruck. It's hard to imagine superwoman Goldie, who lives in a mini mansion in Putney, spending her childhood in a run-down estate. I wonder whether it's no coincidence that we've ended up here, but I don't say anything.

I jump out of the car and with my hands in my pockets stride over towards the block. There's an external staircase and corridors leading to each flat, so after a quick glance around me, I run up the stairs to the second floor and stride towards Flat 6. There is a window to the side of the door rendering the interior invisible due to an ugly net curtain. A light is on in the flat, but try as I can, I can't see through. With a pounding heart, I knock on the door.

There's no answer. I try again, and then I rap on the window. Silence. This is such an unlikely place to keep two kidnapped girls. It's too residential, and if they screamed, someone would hear them. It really doesn't make sense. But then just because Braun bought a bike for this Anthony White doesn't mean he's involved in the kidnap. We do need to find him, though, because he might be able to explain what Braun has been up to. Also, I've got this niggling feeling that the man Rose was seeing might be the same person. Just a sensation in my gut, something I can't ignore. I walk back downstairs and get into Goldie's car, which she's double-parked around the corner.

'No one there, and no name on the exterior of the flat to suggest who lives there. I don't think they're here, Goldie.'

'Look!' Goldie exclaims, staring into her rear mirror and then turning to point at a car driving past us. 'That's Braun!'

'Really?' I turn to look, and yes, it is his fancy car. What is he doing here? Goldie has her hand on the door and is about to get out.

'No!' I say, reaching over to grab her. 'Stay in the car, and let's see what he does, who he meets. Where has he been all of these hours, and why is he here now? If you confront him now, we may never find out.'

'He's my husband,' Goldie murmurs.

'I know,' I say softly. 'This is so messed up.'

Goldie settles back into the driver's seat, and we watch as Braun drives slowly past and then parks on a single yellow line just in front of us. He hurries out of the car, locking it behind him, and then sprints towards block seventeen. Thank goodness he doesn't clock Goldie's car, which being new, big and electric stands out like a sore thumb around here. Just as I did, he runs up the external staircase and hammers on the door to number six. When he doesn't get an answer, he hurries back down the stairs. He looks dishevelled and harassed, clearly agitated, running his fingers through his hair, rubbing his nose, his face contorted with worry. We watch as he gets back into his car.

'We need to follow him,' I suggest. Goldie nods and starts the engine.

'What if he sees us?' she asks.

'I think he's too distracted, but if he does, we'll deal with it then. Let's see where he's going.'

Braun drives fast, and at times I wonder if Goldie will lose him, but she's determined, her jaw set forwards, her fingers tightly gripped around the steering wheel. We go through a couple of amber lights, get hooted at by a van, but all the time, Braun's car is up ahead. Eventually he turns into an industrial estate. As we weave through it, past more modern units near the entrance, the estate becomes increasingly run-down. Eventually Braun swings to the right and pulls up in front of a red-brick building. Some of the windows are broken, and the place looks like it's ready to be pulled down. We watch as Braun gets out of his car and strides inside.

What is he doing here?

27

ROSE

Carly is asleep, but there's no hope of me drifting off. The mattress is both hard and lumpy, and it smells disgusting, of dried-up piss and stale nicotine. The sleeping bag stinks too, but I smooth it over Carly to keep her warm. I can't just lie here doing nothing. I need to try to get us out of this place, to escape from Tony and tell the police exactly what he's done to us. It's ironic how I've seen the cops as the enemy. I rather wish I hadn't because I sure as hell need them now. I've no idea how long I lie there, but eventually I get up and pace the room. There's nothing here that could be of use to me to help get us out.

I haul myself up onto the high windowsill and try both windows. One of them opens a little bit, but it's dark outside, and I've no idea how high up we are. Quite high, I reckon. I'll have to look again in the morning. Perhaps there'll be people around then, and I can shout for help. I shake the metal girders and a pipe that runs up the wall, but everything is fixed properly.

And then I try the door again. I can't hear any voices now, and I wonder if they've left us. The door is properly locked, but I've studied YouTube videos, and I think I know how to pick a lock. At least I managed the one to Mum's filing cabinet at home. I've never actually tried a door before. But I don't have any paperclips or even a pen to try to wedge into the lock. As I pace the room again, wondering if all hope is gone, I notice the rubbish bin lying on its side in the corner. It's bent out of shape and made out of wire.

I sit cross-legged on the floor and try to unpick the wires. It's slow work, and my right index finger is bleeding by the time I've untangled a section of wire and bent it backwards and forwards many times until it eventually snaps. Now I have a little piece about two inches long. Feeling hopeful for the first time, I walk back to the door and try to remember how to pick the lock. I wriggle the wire inside the lock, but nothing happens. This is so frustrating. I wonder if I need a thicker piece. It's getting light now outside, and the grey murky light makes the room look even more dingy than it felt in the dark. And then suddenly, just as I think I might be getting somewhere, the door is flung open, and I literally fall forwards.

Strong fingers grip my shoulders, and an arm snakes around my neck.

'What the hell do you think you're doing, little girl?' Tony asks. He's not wearing his balaclava now, and his arm is so tight around my neck, I think he's going to suffocate me. I try to scream, but it comes out hoarse.

He then releases me and grabs me by the shoulders again and shakes me. Literally shakes me so hard I want to be sick. 'You behave; otherwise you and that kid are going to get hurt. Do you understand?'

'Why are you doing this?' I ask as I try to stop the tears from flowing. 'I thought we were friends, partners?'

'You totally got the wrong end of the stick there, didn't

you? Why would I want to cosy up to a seventeen-year-old kid?'

'How do you know my age?' I've never told him; I wanted him to assume I was much older. He just grunts in response. I read somewhere that you need to keep your captor talking, but I don't know what to say to Tony. He's betrayed me and used me and...

Suddenly there are loud footsteps running up the stairs, and someone rushes into the room. But it's dark in here, and I can't see into the shadows.

'What the hell!' Tony says, noticing him a second before I do. But then it feels as if my heart is going to burst out of my chest.

'Daddy!' I scream as I try to dash forwards into Dad's arms. But Tony is too quick and too strong. He's got me in that headlock again.

Dad's mouth opens, and he takes a step backwards. His eyes are all bloodshot, his shirt is hanging out, and he looks like he hasn't slept in a month. He points a finger at Tony. 'Shit, Tony. I've got it all wrong, haven't I?'

'What do you mean?' Tony asks.

'As you weren't answering your phone, I decided to come to your business premises to ask for your help. But you're the kidnapper! You're the person who broke into our home and left that note. You're demanding a million quid.'

Tony laughs. I try to struggle to get out of his grip, but he just squeezes me tighter. 'I'm not your f-ing nursemaid, Braun. You can't come running to me every time you get into a little scrape. Just because I helped you when you crashed your car with that girl in it doesn't mean I'm your friend. You still owe me, mate. You didn't pay up when I asked for more money, and you've got to pay somehow. Thought I'd be doing you a favour by getting you to pay like this.'

'Let go of my daughter!' Dad yells, and he rushes towards

us. For one fleeting millisecond I believe that everything's going to be alright, that Dad is going to rescue me. But no.

Tony tightens his grip around my neck, so much so that I can't breathe. He tugs me backwards into the shadows, and I start seeing flashing lights and stars, my world turning black. But then I hear the splintering sound of glass and a horrific thud. Tony's grip eases slightly, and as my vision comes back, I scream. Dad's lying there on the floor, totally still, and I think there's dark blood seeping from his head.

'No!' I shout.

'Oh, shut up!' a female voice says. She steps out of the shadows towards Tony and me.

'What are you doing here?' I ask Lauren in a choked voice. None of this makes sense. Tony betrayed me, but what's Lauren got to do with anything? She was meant to be gone from our lives for ever, and now she's here with him. 'You must help Dad. You've got to save him!'

Tony laughs. 'You, young lady, need to get back into your prison cell.'

'Why are you doing this?' I ask.

'If you recall, it's all your own idea. You suggested you were kidnapped, and we're just carrying out your instructions.'

'But Carly's involved now. I didn't mean to get her involved. You need to let her go.'

'It's a bit late to be worrying about that,' Lauren snaps. She's also dressed in all black, and her face is contorted into a sneer. 'You've brought everything down on your own head. You framed me as a thief, you were happy to use Tony when it suited you, and now, if your dad is dead, well, that's all your fault.'

'No!' I scream. 'You need to help him. Please!'

Lauren laughs.

'Come on, troublemaker,' Tony says. I can hear Carly

crying now, and I just hope she doesn't get off the mattress and come out here and see Dad dead on the floor. Is this really my fault? No. I didn't want to be actually kidnapped. This was meant to be a bit of a laugh. Tony drags me back into the room. Carly is sitting up, and she holds her arms out when she sees me. Tony gives me a shove, and I stumble towards the mattress, flinging my arms around Carly. I'm not sure who is comforting who now. And then I watch as he pulls the door to, and I hear the lock from the other side. I pick Carly up and jiggle her on my hip, carrying her across the room to the door. Is Dad going to be okay? What are they going to do to us? And how do Tony and Lauren know each other? None of this makes sense.

I can hear Tony and Lauren talking.

'Shush, sweetie,' I whisper to Carly. 'Can you be quiet a moment so I can listen to what they're saying?'

Sweet little Carly nods at me. I lean my right ear against the door.

'You realise we're going to have to kill them all now, don't you?' Tony says, and I feel my legs give way from underneath me.

28

SIMONE

'I can't believe it,' Goldie whispers. Her hand is shaking so violently, she almost pokes her eye out when she tries to remove a lock of hair from her face. 'You were right. Braun is responsible for this. How can he kidnap his own child, try to destroy me and his parents, for money? He could have just asked me, and I'd have done my best to work out how we could help him. Do you think he's got a gambling problem?'

I shrug, because I'd have thought that as his wife she would be more likely to know than me. But it goes to show that my gut feeling was right. That Braun is a bad man. His moral compass must be so off it's deeply shocking. Poor Rose and poor Carly. The only positives I can draw from this is that the girls are unlikely to come to any harm. However evil Braun may be, I find it hard to believe he would hurt his own daughter.

'Drive around the corner,' I suggest. 'We don't want Braun seeing us if he comes back out. We need some time to think.'

Goldie starts the car up, and I'm glad it's silent and won't draw any attention. She drives slowly around the side of the brick building, and we see two other vehicles. A motorbike and a white van with blacked-out windows.

'Park behind that shed,' I say. 'We don't want them to see your car.'

'He's not alone,' Goldie murmurs. 'It makes it even worse that he's in cahoots with other criminals. Do you think that's the motorbike that Braun bought?'

'I can't be positive, but I think it is.'

And then two men, both dressed in black, come out of a metal door. They stand to the side of the van, their backs to us. If they turn around, I'm sure they'll see the car, and then it could be all over for us too.

'Get down,' I gesture to Goldie. 'We don't want them to see us.'

We slide down our seats, but I can still just about see their faces. The shorter of the two men turns around, and I glimpse his face. I'm sure I recognise him and the red bike. I think it's the man who was waiting for Rose that evening. I wonder if I should say something to Goldie, but now I feel bad for not mentioning it at the time. Besides, it was speculation. He could have just been casing the joint, and when he saw me at the window, he rode off. The taller man throws his hands in the air and tugs open the driver's door to the van, jumping inside.

'We need to write down the number plate,' I say, grabbing my phone and taking a photograph of the van. Then the vehicle starts up and accelerates so hard, the tyres spin. The van disappears from view within a second. The other man, the one I think I recognise, goes back inside, letting the door slam behind him. I also take a photo of the number plate of the bike.

I let out an audible sigh of relief. 'That was close. If they'd turned around, they would have seen us.'

'What are we going to do now?' Goldie asks. 'We know that man is inside; we saw Braun go in. Shall we follow?'

'I think it's time to call the police,' I suggest.

'But the note–'

'If Braun is behind this, then the note doesn't mean anything. It's possible that the girls aren't even here.'

'Braun will go to prison,' Goldie mutters.

It's a bit late to worry about that, but I don't say anything.

'Do you agree that I should call the police? I'm not prepared to take any further risks for Carly's sake,' I say. I bite my bottom lip until it bleeds as I think about Rob and how he has no idea about the horrors that have unfolded. I'm meant to be supporting him and protecting Carly. I've failed terribly.

'Do it,' Goldie whispers.

I dial 999.

'Which service do you need?' the operator asks.

'Police. It's extremely urgent. There's a kidnapping in progress, and two young girls have been taken. They need to come to–' I turn to Goldie. 'Can you look up on the satnav what the address is here?' She finds our current location, and I read it out to the operator. 'Please send the police straight away; it's urgent.'

'What is your name and phone number, please?'

But I don't answer because, in case that note was real, I don't want to risk the kidnappers tracing the police arrival back to me. I hang up.

'Are they coming?' Goldie asks.

'I hope so. Let's park the car around the other side of the building so it's not seen, and wait for the police to come. I just pray they're quick.'

29

ROSE

I've got to do something. I can't just stay in here waiting for Tony and Lauren to shoot us or however else they intend to kill us. And Dad, my lovely dad who came to rescue me, is lying on the other side of the door in a pool of blood. I think he's dead. How could Lauren do that? She must have brought a bottle down on his head because there was shattered glass on the floor. What has he ever done to her? I mean, they used to like each other. I saw how she fluttered her eyes at him and how he smiled at her, leaving his hand on her arm just a little too long. It was gross. Not that he'd ever cheat on Mum. No, Dad can be a prat, but he's a good man. That's why he's turned up here, our hero and our rescuer. I shove my fist into my mouth because I don't want to cry in front of Carly.

'Are you hungry?' I ask her.

She nods.

I pass her a chocolate bar and a bottle of water, quickly stuffing one of the other bars into my mouth. I wonder if we need to ration how much we have. How long are they going to keep us here for? Will they bring us more food and drink?

Carly has chocolate all over her face. 'Can I brush my teeth?' she asks.

I shake my head. She's so cute, to worry about brushing her teeth after eating chocolate. 'It won't matter for one day,' I reassure her.

I walk over to the windows. I tried to open it last night, but now I can see what I'm doing. I haul myself up onto the windowsill and try the window again. It's tall and flimsy, a single pane of glass, and there's a hole in the very top of it, not that I can reach that. It doesn't open more than a few centimetres, but I think if I really pushed it, it might give way. We're higher up than I thought. There's no way we could jump, and down below it's just a yard with a pile of broken pallets and a couple of rusting dumpster bins. There'd be nothing to break our fall as we landed on the tarmac below. The only positive thing is that there's a ledge the other side of the window, on the exterior. It's quite wide, and there would definitely be enough space for Carly and me to sit on it. We could wait there and hope that someone might see us and rescue us. But this place seems so run-down. There are no cars in sight, and the building opposite is even more derelict. There's no glass in the windows, and it actually looks like it might have been burned out. And that gives me an idea.

I fumble in my jacket pocket, and yes, I've got my lighter. I hop back down from the windowsill and walk around the room. Yes, there's a smoke alarm high up on the ceiling. If this place has got an alarm system, then won't the fire services be notified? I remember how at school, Tommo set the fire alarm off because he was smoking a cigarette in the toilets. We all had to evacuate the building, and the fire brigade turned up even though there wasn't a fire. All my class thought it was great because we were in the middle of a maths exam. We had to do the exam the next day, but at least it bought us a few extra hours of revision time.

I walk back to the mattress.

'Carly, are you feeling very brave?'

'Yes,' she says in a barely audible voice that suggests she's anything but.

'This is all a very big and exciting game,' I say, trying to inject a bit of excitement into my voice. Perhaps I should be an actress after all. 'At the moment the bad guys are keeping us captive, and we need to escape so that the good guys can find us. To do that we're going to need to sit on the window ledge on the outside of the building. It's a long, long way down and too far to jump, so you're going to have to sit very still and wait to be rescued. I'll be right next to you. Do you think you can do that?'

Carly nods, but I'm not sure that she understands the ramifications. What do I know about four-year-old kids?

'I'm going to push the window right open and lift you up there, and you have to sit there and wait for me. You mustn't move at all. This could be the most important thing you've ever done in the whole of your life.'

'Okay,' she whispers.

I climb back up onto the windowsill. I wonder why Tony didn't check the window, or perhaps he did but thought this place is so desolate no one would ever rescue us if we sat outside. Let's hope he's wrong. Using brute force, I push the window, and for a split second I think I'm going to tumble. I grab onto the window frame and haul myself back up, but my heart is pumping faster than it's ever done before. Crap, that was close. But now the window is wide open, and the freezing cold air makes me shiver. Leaving it ajar, I jump back down and hurry across the room to get Carly.

I hold her hand as she gets off the mattress, and we walk together towards the window. It was one thing hauling myself up onto the ledge, it's quite another trying to get her up there. I try using the broken chair, but it just gives way under me. In the end I get her up onto my shoulders, and the brave little mite grabs the ledge, and together we get her onto the sill. On second thoughts, I reckon it's safer for her to stay on the inside whilst I carry out the next stage of the plan.

'Carly, I want you to sit where you are, but you're to look out of the window, okay? Don't look at what I'm doing.' I really don't want to frighten her.

'Okay,' she mutters again. I jump back down from the ledge and pick up the sleeping bag, carrying it to the door. I wedge it a little bit under the door, and then I take the lighter out of my pocket and flick open a flame. When I hold the flame under the fabric, it takes hold immediately. I wait a few moments as the sleeping bag begins to burn; it fizzes, and the smell is disgusting. Then the flames take hold, and there's more smoke, and it's only then I realise what I've done.

Shit.

Tony and Lauren won't be able to get in, but it also means our rescuers won't be able to get in either. And Dad's lying on the floor in the next room. I hope the alarm goes off quickly because if it doesn't, I could have killed us all.

Panic courses through my throat and makes my stomach clench. But there's not much I can do now. We've only got one bottle of water left, and that won't put out this fire. I race over to the mattress, grab Carly's blanket and then run to the window before hauling myself up next to Carly.

'I'm going to go outside first, and then I want you to crawl through the window, and I'll hold you.'

'What's that smell?' Carly asks, but I don't have time to answer her. I swing my legs out of the window and bum shuffle until I'm outside. There's just enough space for me to sit with my legs dangling down. I turn.

'You need to come through now, Carly.'

She goes very, very slowly. And for a moment I wonder if I'll have to grab her because the smoke is building up fast now. Why the hell aren't the alarms going off? I cough. Carly does too. I hold my arms out, and she crawls into them. Very carefully, I help her to sit right next to me.

'What if we fall?' she whispers.

'We're not going to fall,' I say with confidence I don't feel. I put my arm around her and hold her tightly.

And then a high-pitched alarm sounds. It rings and rings, and I've never been so happy to hear a bell in the whole of my life.

30

SIMONE

'What's that noise?' Goldie asks, winding down her car window.

'It sounds like an alarm. A fire or burglar alarm perhaps?'

Goldie gets out of the car, so I do the same. She points towards the entrance we saw Braun slip into. We go cautiously, tiptoeing in the shadows of the building just in case there are cameras we haven't noticed or anyone is looking out of a window. The place seems deserted, so I step away from the building and into the road that runs between the derelict warehouse and the one where Braun is.

I look upwards, and then I gasp.

'Up there!' I shout. 'The girls are up there, and there's smoke coming out behind them.' Goldie rushes to my side and looks up. They're sitting on a narrow ledge about three storeys high.

'Rose!' Goldie shouts.

We can't hear Rose's response, but she waves her arms at us.

'The building is on fire!' Goldie exclaims, utter panic on her face. 'For God's sake, don't move, Rose!'

There's no time to waste. Whoever is inside is not going to stay in a burning building. They're going to come out, and the chances are they'll exit via the door that we saw the men go in and out of.

'Stay here, Goldie!' I instruct her.

'Where are you going?'

But I don't have time to answer her. This is our chance, and I have to get to the side of the building. I run. Just around the corner, there's a discarded pallet lying next to a broken car tyre. With strength that I didn't know I had, I rip off a section of wood, ignoring the splinters in the palms of my hands. Then I race to the door, checking where the hinges are, and I stand right up against the wall, ready for whoever comes out. The whole of my body is throbbing with terror, my heart pounding, and I have to force myself to breathe. I hold the piece of wood upwards and out, in front of me. And then it happens.

The door swings open, I step forwards, and I bring it down as hard as I can over the man's head. It's the man we saw earlier, and I let out a little whisper of relief that it's not Braun because, despite everything, I don't know how Goldie would react if I killed her husband. The man's legs give way, and he slumps down onto the tarmac, bashing his head against the brick wall. I stare at him, horrified at what I've done. I've never hurt anyone before, I can't even bring myself to kill a spider, yet I may just have killed another human being. But then I remember, I'm doing this for Carly. I prod at his unconscious form and watch for a moment as blood seeps from the side of his head. Then swallowing bile, I grab his ankles and pull him away from the doorway. I can't think about this man. I need to do it all over again for when the next person comes out, quite possibly Braun. I stand again with the now bloodied piece of wood and hold it up, waiting. The alarm is deafening. I wait. And wait. But no one comes out. Where is Braun? Has he left via another door? And then I have a moment of horrific doubt. What if I've killed the wrong person? What if this man crumpled at my feet is nothing to do with the abduction of Carly and Rose?

I wait another long moment, and then abandoning the piece of broken pallet, I sprint back to the side of the building to join Goldie. She's shouting up at Rose.

'Stay still, Rose. The emergency services are coming!' Goldie shouts.

'You have to go in! Dad's inside, and he's hurt. You've got to rescue him.' Rose is crying, and she looks so vulnerable with her arms around Carly. Smoke is billowing out from various windows now, and I wonder how long we've got until the windows explode and Rose and Carly are hurt.

'I've called the fire brigade and the police,' Goldie says. 'But I need to rescue Braun.'

'You can't go in!' I exclaim.

'I have to.'

'No, Goldie!' I try to grab her arm, but she's too quick for me, and then she's racing in the direction I've just come from.

'Mum!' Rose screams.

'We're getting help,' I shout up at her. 'Hang on in there. Help is coming.'

I follow Goldie, but she's disappeared inside the building, and I just pray that she will be alright. I pick up the piece of wood once again and stand over the man at my feet, just in case he wakes up. I really hope I haven't just murdered an innocent stranger. Time stands still. I try to keep my mind blank, but terror grips me. My breathing is shallow and my heart pumping so loudly it sounds like gunshots in my ears. Please let the girls be alright. Please, emergency services, hurry up. A noxious burning smell wafts downwards, and I hear a crashing noise coming from inside the building. Or did it come from this building; perhaps it was from some-where further away? And then I hear sirens that get louder and louder. I sob as a wave of relief makes me bend double. At least the girls have a chance of being rescued.

31

GOLDIE

I t's pure instinct. I know it's crazy to run into a burning
building, but what choice do I have? I need to save my
daughter and my husband. Braun may be an idiot, but I
love the man. He's the father of my children, and whatever
stupid mess he's got himself into financially can be sorted.
He's too young to die. The children need him; I need him.

In front of me there's a steep concrete staircase. I bound
up it two steps at a time. There's only the hint of smoke in
here, but nevertheless, I tug the scarf off my neck and wrap it
haphazardly around my face, covering my nose and mouth.
What is it you're meant to do in a fire? Crouch down low? I
carry on upwards, and then I'm on a landing, and there's a
dark door in front of me. Just as I'm about to brace myself and
open it, it swings open towards me. Smoke swirls outwards
towards me.

'Braun?'

But it's not Braun.

'What are you doing here?' I step backwards towards the
wall as Lauren comes into the hallway, letting the door slam

behind her. She's coughing, swiping at the smoke ineffectively. For now, the door is keeping the smoke away.

'Where's Braun?' I ask, with mounting panic, totally confused as to why she's here.

'Dead, I hope,' she says as she swipes at her red eyes.

'Why are you here? What have you done?'

'Getting revenge, having fun,' she says with a smile that sends ice through my veins.

'What do you mean?'

'Have you seen Tony?'

'The man who came out of the building?' I'm really struggling to understand what's going on here.

'Don't you know him?' she asks with a sneer.

I shake my head.

'He's your husband's drug dealer and fixer. And now thanks to the introduction via Braun, he's my boyfriend. So where's the money, then?'

I stare at her.

'Don't be so naïve, Goldie. It's me behind the kidnapping plot. Tony's also owed money by your husband, and we're going to split the ransom money. If you think you're going to get out of here without giving us the dosh, you've got another think coming. We'll find you somehow. Get out of my way. I need to go and join him.'

'No,' I say, putting my arm out to stop her from barging past me.

'Don't know why you're so bothered with Braun. Tony treats me way better than he ever did. I'm sure you could do better too, although you're such a bitch, perhaps not.'

'What do you mean?'

'Braun and I were having an affair for ages. But when that brat of a daughter of yours framed me for theft, what did he do? Nothing. He didn't stand up for me; he just let me go despite telling me he loved me and that we had a future together. Thankfully for me, Tony is way more of a man than Braun will ever be.'

I stare at her. The smoke is swirling upwards now from underneath the dark door, making me cough. My eyes are smarting, my heart pounding with shock. And then she laughs, putting her face just centimetres from mine.

'For a woman who thinks she's so bright, you're totally clueless, Goldie.'

And then to my utter relief, I hear sirens. They're almost as loud as the alarm.

'Get out of my way,' Lauren says as she barges past me, roughly pushing me against the wall. I think I'm going to fall, but as I flail my arms around to catch my balance, my elbow catches Lauren on the back of her head. It's Lauren who tumbles downwards, a scream echoing through the concrete stairwell. I hesitate for a moment, but I don't have time to check if she's alright. I need to rescue my husband.

I swing open the door, shouting Braun's name. The smoke is so dense I can't see a thing, and the heat is like the inside of an oven racing towards me. With my arms held out in front of me, I bend down low, edging forwards. And then I trip, and I tumble right on top of a soft body.

Braun.

I can't see anything, my eyes are streaming, and I'm coughing, spluttering, inside my scarf. I fumble to find his hands and instead realise his feet are facing towards me. Grabbing his ankles, I pull him as I step backwards, my breathing becoming increasingly difficult, the acrid smoke burning the back of my throat, the insides of my nostrils. I can't find the door now, and I realise that it might only be seconds until I'm overcome by smoke. Don't let me die! Please don't let me die. Rose and Florian need us.

And then strong arms grasp me, and I'm hauled over a shoulder. I'm coughing and spluttering, and it feels as if my lungs are going to explode. But seconds later I'm outside the building, surrounded by firemen and policemen and paramedics. And in amongst the strangers and the blue lights and the mayhem is Simone. I drop down to my knees as I gulp in the fresh air.

'They're rescuing Rose and Carly right now,' she says, bending down to talk to me. 'They've got a ladder up there. The girls are safe.'

I sob.

'And Braun, is he alive?'

We both watch as a fireman exits the building with Braun over his shoulder. Paramedics rush forwards, so many people it looks like a crowd, and then they're covering his face with an oxygen mask, working on him.

'I don't know,' I whisper, but utter exhaustion settles over me, and I don't have the strength to go to him, to find out if he's alright. I just blurt it out, 'Braun had an affair with Lauren.'

'Lauren?' Simone's mouth drops open. 'Lauren who used to work for you? What's she got to do with anything?'

'She's the woman over there, on that stretcher. She's with that man called Tony. He's a drug dealer, and he's also Lauren's new boyfriend.' A sob turns into a cough, the smell and taste of smoke bitter and burning in my throat.

I can see that Simone is struggling to keep up, and it's no surprise.

'Is Tony the man that I may or may not have killed?' she asks.

'Yes.' I glance over to the stretcher where they're treating Tony, and they're lifting him up into the ambulance, an IV in his arm. 'He's still alive, by the looks of things.'

I stagger back to my feet. I need to see Rose, to put my arms around my daughter, to make sure she's alright.

'Which one of you is Simone?' a policeman asks. 'Because little Carly is asking for you.' Simone rushes away.

I can't move so quickly, but I stagger forwards, just desperate to be with my girl. What a terrible, terrible mess.

32

SIMONE

It's night-time, and I'm at the hospital. We all are; we've been here for hours, along with a big police presence. A police officer rescued Minnie from my car and took her to Braun's parents. They've been taking statements from Goldie and me and Rose. I suppose they'll do the same with Braun, Lauren and Tony when they're well enough. I've been interviewed at length by a policeman called DS Colin Stewart. I asked for PC Deidre Withington to be present because she was so kind when we got the news that Ally died. She's not part of the team, apparently. I've told DS Stewart the truth, that I got the job with the Deluccis under false pretences because I was convinced there was more to Ally's death than met the eye. He just looked at me as if I was deranged. That was why I wanted Deidre Withington there because I always got the sense that she was on my side. I guess she's not senior enough in the police hierarchy, or in the right division, for her opinion to count. DS Stewart is satisfied with my statement and has let me go, as has the presiding doctor, who gave me a thorough check over for smoke inhalation. Of course I didn't have any. It was Goldie who really suffered.

They've also kept Carly in hospital for observation, and that's where I am right now. At her bedside, stroking her hair as she sleeps. The paediatrician said she doesn't expect Carly to suffer any long-term trauma, but she should definitely get counselling, not just for the loss of her mother but also for the terrifying experience of the kidnapping and fire. She promised that if Carly is treated now whilst she's so little, there'll be no long-term consequences. I just pray she's right because it's all my fault. I'm going to have to tell Rob the truth, and I'm absolutely dreading that.

Carly is in a private room. It's small, yet she looks tiny in the big bed with the grey plastic sides, but her face is so peaceful. I'll stay here all night, right next to her, until she wakes up and I can take her home.

It's gone 8 pm when there's a gentle knock at the door.

'Come in,' I say quietly. Carly doesn't stir.

I'm surprised to see Rose. Her face is tear-stained and her hair wet.

'I'm so sorry, Simone,' Rose says, clenching and unclenching her hands in front of her. She's wearing a pink sweatshirt that dwarfs her. I assume they've taken away her clothes. 'It's all my fault, and I can't believe I got Carly involved in this. She's such a sweet kid, and I might have ruined her life.' Simone swipes away a tear.

'You haven't ruined her life, Rose. And besides, it's not your fault. Tony and Lauren organised the kidnapping. They're the ones who have been arrested and will eventually be going to jail.' I am so shocked by Lauren's involvement. It still doesn't make sense to me, but mostly I'm saddened by my own lack of judgement. I genuinely liked her, yet I got her utterly wrong. Perhaps I was so desperate to get information to fit my theory, I didn't care who I used along the way.

'Yes, it is my fault,' Rose interrupts my thoughts. 'I suggested the kidnapping to Tony, and he ran with it but made it real. And I know who you are too. The policeman told me.' She turns away from me and balls her fists. 'The thing is, I think Dad might have had something to do with your sister's death. Tony mentioned it. I don't know exactly how he was involved, but I think he was.'

I stare at the floor, the pattern on the blue linoleum that blurs the more I look at it. So I might have been right all along.

'Have you been to see your dad?' I ask Rose.

She shakes her head. 'He came out of surgery about an hour ago. Mum's with him, and I'll see him later. He's going to be okay though.'

I stand up. 'Would you mind staying here for a few minutes and keeping an eye on Carly?'

'Sure,' Rose says. 'Can I stroke Carly's hair?'

'Of course you can.'

I WALK DOWN the corridor and out of the paediatrics wing into the body of the hospital. At the main reception, I get directions for where Braun is staying, and I just hope they'll let me in to see him. As I'm at the entrance to the ward, DS Colin Stewart is coming out.

'I really need to talk to Braun Delucci. Can you persuade the nurses to let me in? I think you might want to hear the conversation.'

He throws me a strange glance, but credit to him, he doesn't question me. A moment later, the nurse is leading me along a corridor and knocks on the door of another private room. I'm relieved that Goldie isn't there.

'You've got another visitor, Mr Delucci,' the nurse says. 'He's still a bit woozy, but he's going to be fine.' She smiles at me and leaves the room. DS Stewart stands in the corridor out of sight, his back against the wall. I leave the door ajar so that he can hear what we're saying.

As I walk into the room, Braun turns his head towards me, and his eyes widen when he sees me. He has a bandage around his head, and his arm is in plaster.

I don't beat around the bush. 'I know what you did. I know that you had an affair with Lauren and that Tony was your drug dealer.' Of course I don't know any of this for sure, but I'm taking an educated guess.

'There's no crime in any of that,' Braun says, surprisingly articulate for someone who has just come around from a general anaesthetic.

'You bought drugs, Braun! That's a crime.'

'Look, I'm the good guy here, trying to rescue my daughter and your niece. I'm not sure what you're getting at, Simone.'

'I don't buy that for one second. You said you knew my references were fake, but do you know who I really am?'

He frowns at me, and from the way he winces, I can tell the movement is painful. I'm glad.

'My name is Simone Carver, and I'm Alison Greystone's sister. I know what happened the night you left the studio with Ally.' I don't, but I'm pulling off the biggest bluff of my life because after what Rose told me, I am utterly positive that Braun was involved. 'You can tell me in your own words, or I'll just go and talk to DS Stewart, who is waiting out in the corridor.'

I swallow hard, my heart pounding.

Braun's face turns a pale grey, and he turns his head away from me. His voice is hoarse and subdued. 'She was such a lovely girl. I'd always fancied Ally, but she wasn't having any of it. I persuaded her to get a lift with me that night. It was late, and she was exhausted, and well, I thought something might happen now filming was over. I'd taken drugs, I mean we all do, don't we?'

I feel like screaming at him, saying no we don't, but I clench my fists and let him carry on talking.

'I was high. High on drugs and on adrenaline for wrapping the film. It was pissing with rain, and I lost control of the car. I didn't mean for any of it to happen. It was an accident. The car slammed into a tree, and whilst I was fine, I could see that Ally wasn't. You've got to understand that I was in a total panic. It was pitch black, no other cars around. We were in a ditch, and what was I meant to do? I called Tony. Yes, he's my dealer and a bit of a fixer. Tony tipped up quickly, took one look at Ally and said she wouldn't survive. So what was the point in killing off both of us? If I'd turned myself in, that would have been the end of my life; my family would have been destroyed along with Delucci Productions. All those people and investors dependent on me and Goldie.' His voice fades away.

I feel like throwing up. Instead, I sink into my haunches with my back up against the wall.

'Tony and I moved Ally into the driver's seat, and then Tony injected her with meths. Afterwards, he pushed the car a bit further off the hillside. It was all him. I was in such a state I didn't know what the hell was going on. Tony took me to the editing suite then. I was such a screw-up. Anyway, Martin was there, and he helped get me cleaned up. He didn't know what had happened, obviously, but I persuaded Martin to give me an alibi. You see, it was all Tony's idea, and I just left him to it. I owe him a lot of money for cleaning up my mess, and he keeps on coming back asking for more. But he's the one who's responsible. Not me. It was an accident, Simone. You see that, don't you?'

Braun's voice peters out, and I'm glad his head is still turned away from me. I stand up. I expect he's waiting for me to say something, to exonerate him perhaps, tell him that of course it's all Tony's fault. But I say nothing. Instead I walk straight out of the door.

By the look on DS Stewart's face, I can tell he heard every word.

'I've recorded it on my phone,' I say, holding it out to him. 'I need to take Carly home to her dad now.'

'Of course, And thank you, Simone.'

33

SIMONE – A YEAR LATER

I've never been to a premiere before, but Goldie was insistent that Rob and I attend. She even offered to buy me a new dress, but that was a step too far. I've rented one. It's silver and sequinned, and I feel a million dollars in it. Rob opens the door to the taxi, looking dapper in an evening suit. I know that Ally would have been so proud of him. His heart is still shattered, but he is trying incredibly hard to pull himself together, religiously attending counselling sessions and avoiding any alcohol. As for me, well, frankly, I'm terrified about this evening.

Goldie is standing at the far end of the red carpet, wearing a long black dress embellished with feathers. I'm surprised to see Rose and Florian standing next to her. Florian's face lights up when he sees me. Rob takes my arm, and we walk towards them. I try hard to ignore the flashing bulbs of the photographers, but it's extremely off-putting. I know they're not interested in me, but even so, I feel self-conscious. This is, after all, the Odeon in London's Leicester Square, where many leading films preview.

'Simone,' Goldie says, stepping forwards and kissing me

on both cheeks. 'You look stunning.' That does get the paps flashing.

'As do you.'

We all walk inside the cinema and take our seats on the front row. I have a handbag stuffed with tissues, and yes, I do need them. It's quite possibly the hardest thing I will ever do, watching Ally up there on the big screen. She is – or should I say was – magnificent in *The Insomniac*, and I quickly forget that I'm watching my sister, instead losing myself in her mesmerising character. But when the film ends, I have no hope of keeping my eyes dry. The words on the screen say:

> *This film is dedicated to Alison Greystone, mother, wife, actor, taken from us much too soon.*

The words swim in front of my eyes. I glance over at Goldie, who is holding a handkerchief to her face. Except for the gentle music, there is silence in the auditorium. And then the audience starts clapping, and as I glance behind me, I see that many of the people in the auditorium have risen to their feet. Some of the cast are in the row behind us, and Kit blows me a kiss. I just pray that Ally is watching from heaven, that she knows how much people appreciated her.

The media presence in all of our lives has been intense, but none more so than for Goldie. Braun is still being held in custody, awaiting his trial. It's taken so long, and we all just wish it could be over and done with. Many journalists thought that *The Insomniac* should be shelved, but the crew and cast were in uproar about it. In the end, Goldie asked me and Rob to be the arbiters. We were unanimous. It must be released. It's the final tribute to my beautiful sister.

The trials of Lauren and Tony took place just last month. Lauren has been sentenced to eight years in jail, which seems a very short time for someone involved in the kidnap of two children. I'll never know for sure whether the hand on my back was hers, but I suspect it might have been Lauren who tried to push me into the road. I accept I will never know the truth because I have no intention of visiting her in prison. But you won't find me standing anywhere near the edge of a road or a railway platform ever again.

Tony has been wanted by the police for a long time for drugs offences and is now on trial for kidnapping, blackmail and murder. It's likely he'll get life in prison, although he'll probably be released after twenty years or so. Hopefully not. Martin is also on trial for perverting the course of justice, but his trial will take place after Braun's. I feel an iota of sympathy towards Martin, who was put in an impossible situation. I hope the jury go lightly on him.

After a minute, the music gradually fades, and the rest of the credits scroll up on the big screen. The filmgoers leave the auditorium, and it's just the Deluccis and us left behind.

'What are you going to do now?' I ask Goldie as we follow Florian and Rose out of the cinema.

'I'm divorcing Braun. The house is on the market, and we'll move somewhere smaller. We're in the final stages of negotiating the sale of Delucci Productions, and we'll get some money from it, because the funding is complete for *What She Knew*, and the film will go ahead. But I'm taking a step backwards. I will have some limited involvement in the business going forwards, but my priority now is the children. They should have always been my priority.'

'Have you recruited a new concierge?' I ask.

She laughs. 'No. There's no need. So if you ever decide you want to return to the position, I'm afraid I can't offer you a job, but I'll give you the very best references.'

Now it's my turn to chuckle. 'I think I'll give that one a miss. My business is going well, and I have a new boyfriend who lives in Brighton. I'm thinking of moving down there, and Rob is seriously considering relocating with Carly too.'

We're interrupted then by a PR woman, who ushers Goldie away to talk to the waiting journalists. I don't know how she does it, keeping strong in light of the terrible things that have happened.

Rob puts his arm around my shoulders. 'Actually, I've found a house. I'll show you the particulars later.'

'Sorry to be eavesdropping,' Rose says, slowing down so she's level with us. 'But will there be a room for me so I can come and babysit Carly?'

'There'll always be a place for you in Carly's life,' Rob says.

'Even though it was all my fault, and I might have traumatised her for life?'

'You haven't,' Rob says.

'And it wasn't your fault,' I quip. 'I never even told Rob where I'd taken Carly, so I was equally to blame.'

'This is a new chapter in all of our lives,' Rob says.

'Mine too,' Florian murmurs. We turn to look at him. 'I've persuaded Mum to send me to a new school.'

I give Florian a quick hug, and then we say our goodbyes. The press are no longer interested in Rob and me, so we just disappear into the throng.

A LETTER FROM MIRANDA

Thank you very much for reading The Concierge. The idea for this book was sparked by my curiosity of lifestyle concierge services. I wondered what it must be like organising the lives of time-poor, wealthy people. But as is often the case, this book veered quite far off course and morphed into something rather different. I hope you enjoyed it nevertheless! My wonderful editor, Jan Smith, is also a scriptwriter so I could draw on her experience of working in the film industry. Any mistakes are my own.

I am dedicating this book to the memory of my best friend, Rosamund Smith (1967-1991). According to the World Health Organisation, road traffic accidents continue to be the leading cause of death for young people under the age of 29. I hoped that in the past thirty years, this statistic might have improved but we still have a long way to go to achieve the WHO's target of halving the global number of deaths from traffic accidents by 2030. If you have also lost someone you love this way, my heart goes out to you. We never forget.

It's been a busy year of writing with Inkubator Books and as always, I couldn't have done it without the support from an amazing team. A huge thank you to Brian Lynch, Garret Ryan, Jan Smith, Stephen Ryan, Claire Milto, Alice Latchford, Pauline and the rest of the team.

I owe so much to the book blogging community who take the time to review my psychological thrillers, share my cover reveals and talk about my books on social media. Thank you in particular to CarrieShields (@carriereadsthem_all), Judy Collins (@JudithDCollins) and Zooloos Book Tours along with everyone who takes part. I am so grateful that you share your thoughts on my books.

And finally, and most importantly, thank you, my lovely reader. I still pinch myself every day that I'm a full time writer and that could never have happened if you didn't choose to read my thrillers. Reviews on Amazon and Goodreads help other people discover my novels, so if you could spend a moment writing an honest review, no matter how short it is, I would be massively grateful.

My warmest wishes,

Miranda

www.mirandarijks.com

ALSO BY MIRANDA RIJKS

Made in the USA
Coppell, TX
11 December 2022

88865570R00156